MW00366544

Cover design by Juan Villar Padron,
https://www.juanjpadron.com

Special thanks to my editor Janell Parque
http://janellparque.blogspot.com/

---

To be the first to hear about **exclusive new releases
and FREE ebooks from Willow Rose**, sign up below
to be on the VIP List. (I promise not to share your email
with anyone else, and I won't clutter your inbox.)

- GO HERE TO SIGN UP TO BE ON THE VIP LIST :
http://readerlinks.com/l/415254

**Tired of too many emails?** Text the word: "wil-
lowrose" to 31996 to sign up to Willow's VIP text List to
get a text alert with news about New Releases, Giveaways,
Bargains and Free books from Willow.

HARRY HUNTER MYSTERY - BOOK 1

# ALL THE GOOD GIRLS

## WILLOW ROSE

Books by the Author

## MYSTERY/THRILLER/HORROR NOVELS

- IN ONE FELL SWOOP
- UMBRELLA MAN
- BLACKBIRD FLY
- TO HELL IN A HANDBASKET
- EDWINA

### HARRY HUNTER MYSTERY SERIES

- ALL THE GOOD GIRLS
- RUN GIRL RUN

### MARY MILLS MYSTERY SERIES

- WHAT HURTS THE MOST
- YOU CAN RUN
- YOU CAN'T HIDE
- CAREFUL LITTLE EYES

### EVA RAE THOMAS MYSTERY SERIES

- DON'T LIE TO ME
- WHAT YOU DID
- NEVER EVER
- SAY YOU LOVE ME
- LET ME GO

### EMMA FROST SERIES

- ITSY BITSY SPIDER
- MISS DOLLY HAD A DOLLY
- RUN, RUN AS FAST AS YOU CAN
- CROSS YOUR HEART AND HOPE TO DIE
- PEEK-A-BOO I SEE YOU
- TWEEDLEDUM AND TWEEDLEDEE
- EASY AS ONE, TWO, THREE
- THERE'S NO PLACE LIKE HOME
- SLENDERMAN
- WHERE THE WILD ROSES GROW
- WALTZING MATHILDA
- DRIP DROP DEAD

## JACK RYDER SERIES

- HIT THE ROAD JACK
- SLIP OUT THE BACK JACK
- THE HOUSE THAT JACK BUILT
- BLACK JACK
- GIRL NEXT DOOR
- HER FINAL WORD
- DON'T TELL

## REBEKKA FRANCK SERIES

- ONE, TWO…HE IS COMING FOR YOU
- THREE, FOUR…BETTER LOCK YOUR DOOR
- FIVE, SIX…GRAB YOUR CRUCIFIX
- SEVEN, EIGHT…GONNA STAY UP LATE
- NINE, TEN…NEVER SLEEP AGAIN
- ELEVEN, TWELVE…DIG AND DELVE
- THIRTEEN, FOURTEEN…LITTLE BOY UNSEEN
- BETTER NOT CRY
- TEN LITTLE GIRLS

- It Ends Here

---

## HORROR SHORT-STORIES

- Mommy Dearest
- The Bird
- Better watch out
- Eenie, Meenie
- Rock-a-Bye Baby
- Nibble, Nibble, Crunch
- Humpty Dumpty
- Chain Letter

---

## PARANORMAL SUSPENSE/ROMANCE NOVELS

- In Cold Blood
- The Surge
- Girl Divided

## THE VAMPIRES OF SHADOW HILLS SERIES

- Flesh and Blood
- Blood and Fire
- Fire and Beauty
- Beauty and Beasts
- Beasts and Magic
- Magic and Witchcraft
- Witchcraft and War
- War and Order
- Order and Chaos

- Chaos and Courage

**THE AFTERLIFE SERIES**

- Beyond
- Serenity
- Endurance
- Courageous

**THE WOLFBOY CHRONICLES**

- A Gypsy Song
- I am WOLF

**DAUGHTERS OF THE JAGUAR**

- Savage
- Broken

## Chapter 1

"I DON'T LIKE IT, ROBERT."

"What's that?"

Robert didn't even look up from his laptop. It was late at night, and he was still working, as usual, even on a Friday night.

"I haven't heard from her in hours," Valentina said. "She hasn't responded to any of my texts."

Robert sighed and glared at her from behind the laptop. He was still every bit as handsome as he had been when they met twenty years ago at the annual Vizcaya Ball, which anyone who was anyone in Miami's high society attended. She had been in her early twenties, and he had been ten years older. Still, it seemed like she was the one who looked the oldest these days. He kept himself in shape to a degree that Valentina often worried he might have other women on the side. Robert traveled a lot and was often gone for weeks at a time. Who knew what he did on those business trips?

"It's a dance, Valentina. It's prom. It's a big deal around here, and it is to your daughter too. She won't be

1

keeping an eye on her phone all night, waiting for your texts. Frankly, I would be more concerned if she had answered."

*Around here.*

Robert always said stuff like that condescendingly like she wouldn't understand because she wasn't from *around here*. Because she was from Colombia...because she had come here when she was in her late teens and never attended an American high school. It was something in the way he said it that made her cringe like she wasn't good enough because she wasn't fully American and never would be.

"Well, she promised me she'd text me," she said with a small snort. "And now it's getting really late."

"She's seventeen; she knows how to handle herself."

"I'm not so sure. Those kids at her school, I don't trust them."

That made Robert laugh. "You don't trust anyone, Valentina. It's in your nature."

And there it was again. Always making sure she knew she was different from him. It was something that had grown in their marriage over the years, coming between them...a disdain toward her. Valentina found it to be odd. Living in Key Biscayne, they were surrounded by people from South America...wealthy people who had nannies and drove expensive cars but spoke Spanish. Living there, Robert felt surrounded, invaded almost, and slowly, he had begun to fight to conserve his sense of being a white American. It was important that his daughter knew she was American, he would suddenly say, and he wouldn't have her speak any Spanish, so Valentina had to teach her when he wasn't at home.

"Well, I don't," she said, lifting her nose toward the

ceiling in contempt. "They have never been good to Lucy."

Valentina grimaced when saying the name. It was something they had discussed endlessly when she had become pregnant…what to name their daughter. Valentina wanted to name her a Colombian name; she wanted her to know where she came from, whereas Robert believed she needed to be as American as possible. In the end, Valentina had put her foot down and said she was naming her Luciana after her great-grandmother, and Robert had given in. But over the years, Luciana had become Lucy, and influenced by her father, their daughter insisted that everyone call her that.

Valentina looked at her Rolex, then felt a pinch of deep worry in the pit of her stomach.

"It's eleven-thirty now, and we still haven't heard anything," she said with a slight whimper. "The prom ended at eleven. She was supposed to text us to pick her up."

"They're probably just hanging out after the party," he said, calming her down, or at least attempting to. "You need to relax."

Valentina stared at her phone, checking if there was a signal, then put it down just as the screen lit up. Relief washed over her as she saw her daughter's name on the display. She opened the text.

"They're going to the beach to make a bonfire," she said with light laughter. "She's asking if it'll be okay that she stays out a little later. Guess I won't be going to sleep anytime soon, then."

"Well, there you go," Robert said. "Your daughter is just having a good time for once. High school has not been easy for her, but now she finally seems to be enjoying herself. Don't ruin it with all your worry, please."

# Chapter 2

VALENTINA STARED at the clock on the wall. It was past two o'clock now, and still, there was no news from her daughter. She was getting tired now and wanted to go to bed soon. Robert had turned in, and Valentina had also been dozing off on the couch, waiting to hear from Lucy.

She looked at her phone again, wondering if she should call her and tell her it was time to come home. It wasn't like Lucy to stay out all night like this, and by now, Valentina feared the girl might have been persuaded to drink alcohol or do something worse. Lucy was a good girl and had stayed away from all that stuff, so Valentina didn't understand why she'd start now. She usually wasn't interested in partying, and it had actually taken some effort to persuade her even to go to this dance. Valentina had bought her a beautiful lavender dress, but still, the girl had told her she didn't want to go. But then some weeks ago, she had come home and suddenly told Valentina that she had changed her mind...that some kids from the school had asked if she was going and had been friendly toward her. There was also a boy, she had admitted, who had told her he thought she was cute. Valentina had thought it was wonderful and hoped that things were finally shaping up for her like her mother had wanted for so many years. They had gone through so much bullying and so many bad times with no friends in school that Valentina had thought this was an answer to her prayers.

But she hadn't expected her daughter to stay out so late.

Now, she didn't know what to do. She did know, however, that two o'clock was way too late, and it was time to put a stop to it. She walked up the stairs to her bedroom and woke Robert.

"She hasn't texted yet. I fell asleep, but now I think we need to get her home. It's two o'clock," she said.

Robert sat up in bed and cleared his throat. "Really? That is too late. Call her and tell her I'm on my way."

Robert rose to his feet and found his jeans, then put them on. Valentina was about to call Lucy when Robert's phone on his nightstand rang. They shared a brief look; then, he grabbed it.

"It's her," he said. "It's Lucy."

Valentina breathed, relieved. But the feeling was soon replaced by anger over her daughter's reckless behavior. Lucy knew this was way too late. She was being very irresponsible.

Robert picked up the phone and held it against his ear. A voice could be heard on the other end and was yelling loudly, so Valentina could hear it vividly even if she couldn't make out what was being said. But she did realize the voice didn't belong to her daughter.

Robert's smile froze, and his eyes became steel gray.

"Who is this? WHO is this?"

Robert looked at the display as the connection was lost.

"Who was that?" Valentina asked fearfully. "What did they say? Robert?"

But Robert was unreachable at this point. His nostrils were flaring, his eyes ablaze with anger.

"Robert? Who was that?"

He grabbed his shirt and put it on while running into the hallway and down the stairs without uttering a single word to his wife.

"Robert?" she called after him, but he just continued, rushing out the front door, which slammed shut behind him.

"Robert? ROBERT?"

ONE YEAR LATER

## Chapter 3

"HEY, you! Yes, you, I'm talking to you!"

I approached the guy in the alley. I couldn't see his face or the young girl's face enough to see their eyes or their features, but I didn't have to.

I knew exactly what was happening.

"This girl is no more than a teenager, and you're selling crack to her?" I said. "What kind of a monster does that?"

The lanky guy stared at me in the darkness. The girl saw the chance to take off and ran out of the alley and into the street. I knew she would probably just run around the corner and find another creep who would sell her whatever she was craving, whatever they had her hooked on. I knew I couldn't save her, but I was doing my part to try and clean out the availability.

"W-what the...?" the guy said. His hand slid back inside his hoodie with the small white rock in it. He puffed himself up in front of me.

I stared down at him. It was one of the advantages of being six-foot-eight. Not many felt superior to you, especially not lowlife drug dealers in Overtown Miami. The guy was about to pull out a weapon; I saw the movement of his hand behind his back, where he probably kept it in the waistband of his jeans. It was most likely a knife since most of these Haitian dealers in this part of town couldn't afford a gun. They were also often searched by the cops patrolling the streets and finding a gun on their body would be excuse enough to shoot them.

We all knew the drill around here.

As his hand moved toward the knife behind his back, I moved my arm just enough for my zip-up hoodie to open up so he could see the gun in my holster inside of it. The sight made him let go of the knife. It also made him realize I was a cop if he hadn't already.

"Hand over the goodies," I said. "I'm confiscating them. You're not selling to any more young girls; do you hear me?"

"No way," the guy said with a sniffle, then wiped his nose. He was edgy, and his hand was shaking. It would soon be time for him to have his next fix. He had to sell to other poor souls in order to keep up with his own demand. It was the circle of life around these parts. And it was a never-ending story.

"That girl is someone's daughter; do you know that?" I asked and reached for his hoodie. I grabbed him by the collar and pulled him upward, closer to my face. "Did you get her hooked, huh? Did you introduce her to crack, giving her the first ride for free, so she'd become a lifelong customer, huh? Don't look at me like that; I know your type. Scum of the earth."

I reached into his pocket and pulled the rock out, still holding him by the collar with the other hand.

"Hey, that's mine!" he yelled.

"Not anymore," I said and put him down.

As I did, he took a swing at me. I wasn't expecting it,

and it took me by surprise. His fist slammed into my right eye with such force that I fell backward. The little kid was a lot stronger than I had given him credit for. I roared in pain while the kid jolted forward, trying to get away.

Another awesome part about being this tall, by the way, is that I have very long arms. So, as the kid leaped forward, thinking he'd be able to get away, I simply reached out my right arm and grabbed him by the hoodie, then pulled him backward. His legs were in the air as I pulled him back and threw him down on the pavement with a thud. I then leaned over him and placed my massive fist on his nose, breaking the bone. Blood gushed from it, and he looked at me, confused. I gave him another blow to his face, then reached into his jeans pocket and found another rock that I took before letting him go.

"Might be a chance for you to try something new, make a career move," I said as I let him go. Above me, the warm Florida night was threatening to end in a storm, and I heard thunder in the distance.

"Hey," the kid yelled after me as I walked away. "You can't do this to me."

"I can't?" I said when I reached the end of the alley. "I think I just did."

"It's police brutality!"

That made me laugh out loud as I walked away with both rocks.

"Yeah? Well, good thing I'm off-duty tonight."

## Chapter 4

THE *SERENITY* FOLLOWED the current with its prow facing the open sea, pushed by a gentle landward breeze. They had turned off the engine and lowered the anchor just outside of the marina. Behind them glittered the Miami lights in the dark night, and they could no longer see the yacht club.

The four girls listened to the music the waves made when gently kissing the sides of the boat. It was so quiet out there in the open ocean, one of them, Sandra, thought to herself. She, for one, had longed for such peace of mind for a long time. Her friend, Katelyn, was drinking a soda.

"Should we be heading back?" Georgiana said. It was her father's boat they had borrowed, and she was always so worried her dad would get mad at her. They had told him they were going fishing, even though they had no idea how.

"It's getting late."

"No," the fourth girl, Martina, said with a light laugh. "We're eighteen now. We can do as we please. Our parents don't get to boss us around anymore. I wanna stay out a little longer, please?"

Katelyn watched Sandra finish her soda. Martina gave them a look. "I can't believe we'll be graduating in just a few months, can you?"

"I sure can believe it," Katelyn said and lifted her soda. "I can't wait to…"

Katelyn stopped talking when they all heard a noise coming from behind them. They turned simultaneously to look and spotted someone standing in the stern of the boat, wearing a black diver's wetsuit.

"Who the heck is that?" Georgiana said and rose to her feet, pushing Martina away. "Hey, you! What are you doing on my boat?"

The person remained eerily still and just stood there like it was the most natural thing in the world. Sandra couldn't see a face or make out if it was a man or a woman.

*Could it be someone who's lost?* Sandra thought to herself for a brief second while Georgiana rushed toward the person. *Maybe this person thought it was his own boat? Maybe he couldn't find his way back in the darkness? Maybe he's in some kind of trouble?*

"You can't just crawl on board my father's boat," Georgiana yelled as she almost reached the diver. Too late did she see the harpoon in his hands, not till it was fired and speared through her chest.

Sandra stopped breathing when she saw what happened. Shock rushed through her body in waves, and she found herself completely unable to move. Martina started to scream and instinctively rush toward Georgiana's lifeless body, but as she did, the diver pulled out a knife. It cut through the air with a hiss, cutting into her skin. The blade penetrated her throat, splitting it open, and she too fell to the deck, landing right next to Georgiana.

Seeing this happen to her friends, Katelyn tried to

make a run for it, but the diver had by then pulled out the spear from Georgiana's heart, reloaded the gun, and fired it at her, hitting her in the leg. Katelyn screamed and fell while the diver rushed toward her. Sandra crawled up on the edge of the boat and looked into the dark water beneath. While the diver slit Katelyn's throat, she made the decision.

She closed her eyes and plunged in.

As she landed in the water, she swam for the surface as fast as she could, then spotted the lights from the yacht club. Sandra screamed while trying to swim.

Then she heard the plunge coming from behind her, and panic set in as she realized the diver had jumped in after her. She swam for her life, screaming for help, desperately flapping the water, but feeling like she was going nowhere, like in those awful nightmares she always had where she ran and ran, but never moved. She lifted her head above the water and gasped for air when she felt something grab her. Arms reached up from the ocean beneath her and pulled her downward forcefully into the deep darkness below.

## Chapter 5

"YOU SHOULD HAVE SEEN HER; it was like that time when we told her she couldn't start horseback riding because we couldn't afford it. Do you remember that? Of course, you do. How could you forget? It almost broke your heart, having to say no to her. It was embarrassing to her since Amelia, her best friend, got to go. That's the only time I remember you being embarrassed by us not having much."

I reached over and took Camille's hand in mine. It was so delicate, and I was reminded of the day of our wedding when I had put the ring on her finger. I had held her hand in mine and thought it was such a responsibility to have to take care of another person, someone so fragile.

I had no idea how right I had been.

"Anyway, I told her she was grounded for a month, then took it back and said a week instead. But then she started to bargain, and we ended on two days. I know what you're thinking; don't give me that look," I said and chuckled, then leaned back in my chair, running a hand through my hair. My face was still pounding from the beating I had received the night before. "I am weak; I have to admit it. I have a soft spot for our daughter. I never can be mad at her for more than a few minutes. It's those eyes, you know? I can't resist them."

I sighed and looked at my wife. She was still beautiful, so gorgeous. And those eyes, they still had me locked in. Even though they weren't exactly looking at me, but down at the floor while her head slumped to the side and slid downward toward her shoulder. I grabbed it and pushed it back in place on the pillow. I had bought her one of those elevation beds so she could sit up straight from time to time, but her head kept falling, so I lowered it slightly. Her eyes stared right past me as I looked at her beautiful face and caressed her cheek. I leaned over and wiped drool from her chin, then kissed her cheek gently, closing my eyes, envisioning her when she had still been well.

Before the drugs caused her brain damage.

People usually thought that if you overdosed, you either died or you would be okay. But that wasn't always true. Not for Camille. She had been a drug addict when I met her through my job as an undercover cop at Miami PD, infiltrating the underworld of crack, especially in Overtown, the Haitian part of town. She had been hooked back then, and I had taken her to a rehab facility, taken her off the streets, paying for it out of my own pocket. I had visited her every day while she was there, and soon, we fell in love. When she was released, she moved in with me in my townhouse, and the year after, we were married, and she had our daughter, Josie. For years, she stayed clean; at least I believed she was clean. Until one day three years ago, when I came home from my shift and found her. Her head rested on a pillow on the couch, her wrists were bent and fingers contracted into fists. She was rocking back and forth as if to stand up but then collapsed into the sofa.

That was when I knew something was terribly wrong. She had taken heroin and fentanyl and that had caused her to stop breathing. I rushed her to the hospital, and they managed to get her to breathe on her own again. Her kidneys had failed and they had then recovered as well. But her brain had been starved of oxygen for so long that it was left severely damaged. Now, she lived in the bedroom upstairs in her new bed, while I slept on a mattress on the floor next to her, making sure I'd wake up in case she needed me.

The doctors said she would never be the same as she used to be. Still, I was determined to make the most of our time together while she was still here. But, boy, I missed hearing her voice. I missed hearing her laugh and seeing her dance with our daughter in the kitchen downstairs. I missed everything about her, but most of all, I missed looking into her deep brown eyes. I hated that she was just lying there in that bed, completely lifeless alongside a urinary catheter, pill boxes, and her feeding tube.

"There you go," I said and wiped the last of the drool away, then tossed the napkin, biting back my tears. "You're as good as new."

There was a small knock on the door, and Jean, my next-door neighbor, poked her head in.

"I think Josie is ready for school soon," she said. "I can take over and give Camille her bath now?"

I smiled when seeing her. Jean wasn't only my neighbor; she was also my savior and helping hand. She was a registered nurse and helped me out with Camille as much as I needed. She was also Camille's best friend and had been very close to her before the overdose. At least, we thought she was, but she had been every bit as surprised as I was to learn that Camille had started doing drugs again.

I walked to her and hugged her. "Thank you, Jean.

You're the best. I don't think I would know how to get by without you. I'm sure Camille knows how much you do for her and us, and if she could, she'd thank you."

That made her blush. "Don't give me that," she said and waved me away. "You'll ruin my makeup. I just got myself ready for my shift and all the doctors I plan on flirting with today. I won't have you ruin that. Go and take care of your daughter, and then I'll have a look at that shiner afterward."

## Chapter 6

"GOD, please bless this food and the people eating it."

I held my daughter's hand in mine while saying the prayer, then opened my eyes and looked at her while I added:

"And please help Josie not to be so addicted to her darn phone."

I sent her a look as she realized I had caught her with the phone in her other hand.

"Busted," I said and reached out my hand. "Hand it over—no phones at the table. You know the rules. And especially not while we pray."

"But it's just breakfast, Dad. It's not like it's dinner or anything."

"Hand it over, please."

Josie sighed and handed me the phone. I put it in my pocket, and she gave me a look that told me she didn't think this was fair treatment. I didn't care. She was on that thing all the time. Sitting at the table was the one time I wanted her full attention.

"So, what's up for today?" I asked and served her some eggs and a bagel. "Any big tests?"

She shrugged. "Only math."

"Only math, huh?"

"It's not that hard, Dad."

I stared at my daughter. She was in the eighth grade, doing ninth grade advanced class math. I didn't do that when I was her age. Josie was doing really well in school, something I was certain she got from her mother. Camille could have done anything with her life, and almost did. She went to FIT, Florida Institute of Technology, for engineering and would have finished her education if someone —that being the monster of a boyfriend at the time—had not introduced her to crack one day. After that, she had ended up on the streets of Miami until I picked her up one day when we raided an abandoned building in Overtown. I took one look at her and knew I loved her. I still did, despite it all.

"Really? So you're gonna ace it, I take it."

She smiled cunningly. "Don't I always?"

I chuckled and drank coffee, hoping it might soon kick in so I could feel more awake. I had been out until midnight the night before, while my dad, who lived right down the street, hung out with Josie, so she didn't have to be alone.

"So, what happened to your eye?" she asked while shoveling in eggs. She had a healthy appetite, on the verge of insatiable, which was probably needed in order for her to keep growing the way she did. She was closing in on five feet eleven at the age of only fourteen years old. There was no saying how tall she was going to get. That part, she didn't get from her mother. That was my humble contribution. But that was about it. The rest of her was her mother's spitting image, especially her good looks. Josie was gorgeous beyond what seemed possible. Her creamy caramel skin, her light green sparkling eyes, and thick curly hair made most people compare her to a young Tyra Banks. I'd rather compare her to Camille, the most beautiful woman to have walked this earth, in my eyes.

Only she was too good for it.

"Dad?"

I glared at her. I didn't want to answer her question and explain what I had been up to the night before, so instead, I finished my cup and looked at my watch.

"You should get going," I said as I got up and grabbed both our plates. "Bus leaves in two minutes, and you still haven't brushed your teeth."

## Chapter 7

"OUCH!"

I jumped up. Jean put her hand on her hip and tilted her head. "If you don't sit still, how am I supposed to help you?"

"I don't want your help," I said. "I'm fine."

"Uh-huh, and I'm a secret Russian spy. Now, please sit back down and let me finish this. Your attacker split open the skin above your eyebrow, and I need to close it with these strips. I can't do that if you keep whining. I told you to hold that cold pack on your eye while I fixed this."

I sat back down and tried to relax while pressing the cold pack against my black eye. Jean placed butterfly strips on my skin, pulling it, so it hurt.

"Sit still; I said. Now, tell me something…how did this happen again?"

"It's none of your business," I mumbled.

"None of my business? Right now, it seems to be a whole lot of my business. Patching you up has been all of my business lately. Were you out patrolling the streets on your own again?"

"Maybe?"

"And what exactly does your boss say to you running around the streets at night like some madman, getting beaten up, chasing drug dealers?"

I looked up at her. "He tells me not to?"

"Exactly. Then why don't you stop? You're never going to find the guy that sold Camille those drugs. He's probably dead from an overdose himself anyway."

I grumbled as she placed another strip on my sore skin. "I might not be able to find the guy that did this to Camille, but I can stop others from doing it. I can stop them from selling this stuff to young kids and ruining their lives."

"Uh-huh...and didn't your boss take you out of the narcotics department?" she asked, giving me that look again. Jean had dark blue eyes like me and dark brown hair that she kept in a ponytail so it wouldn't fall in her face while she took care of patients. She was athletically built and a lot stronger than you'd think. She had been my rock through all of this, the past three years, and for that, I owed her everything.

"He did...but..."

"And why do you think he did that, huh, Harry? Was it because you were doing such a great job?"

"No, but..."

"No, he took you off the streets because you couldn't control yourself—because you kept beating people up and get beaten yourself. He was afraid you were going to get yourself killed one day out in those streets. Now, how about you listen to that boss of yours and don't get yourself killed, how about that? Because there are people here who need you, Harry. People who wouldn't get by without you."

"So, focus on the people I still have and don't run,

thinking I can fix things that have already happened, is that what you're saying? Thanks, but we've had this conversation before, Jean, and I still don't think it's any of your business."

Jean answered with a grunt, then finished me up, and then the display on my phone lit up.

"That's the third time this morning," she said. "Don't you think you should answer that?"

I stared at the display, then put it down. "It's just my boss. I'll talk to him when I get there."

## Chapter 8

"NICE OF YOU TO show your pretty face for once."

Major Fowler gave me that look above his glasses. He was sitting behind his desk, looking through a file when I walked in. He glared at his watch for a brief second. "Only two hours late. I think that might be a new record for you, Harry...Geez, what happened to your face? You know what? I have a feeling I don't want to know."

Fowler leaned back in his leather chair. His salt and pepper hair had been cut very short, probably by the same barber he had used forever, even before he and I had become friends twenty years ago when we were both rookies at the Miami-Dade Police Department. Fowler had climbed the career ladder and become a major, while I was still the man on the ground, now serving in the homicide unit.

"Listen, Fowler, I am..."

Fowler lifted both of his bushy eyebrows. "No, Hunter, you listen to me. I can't keep covering for you, making excuses for you. You come and go as you please, and you're never at the briefings in the mornings. I know it's been a tough time for you and your family, and I have given you all the rope I can, but at some point, it has to stop. Frankly, I don't know what to do with you, especially not on a day like today when we need everyone at the top of their game."

"Why? What's going on?"

He threw out his arms. "If you'd been at the briefing this morning, you'd know."

"Or if you tell me now, I'd know too," I said.

He sighed, tapping his pen on the desk. He pulled out a photo from the file and slid it across the desk for me to see.

"Four teenage girls were found dead last night."

He grabbed another photo and showed it to me. "Three of them were found on this boat anchored outside the yacht club; the fourth washed up by the yacht club's seawall. Two of them had their throats slit; one had been harpooned in the heart, while the fourth had drowned. We don't know if she drowned while trying to escape or if someone killed her. They had borrowed the boat from one of their parents and had taken it out to fish, the father said. The first body, the girl that drowned, was found just before midnight by the personnel that was closing down the club for the night. Two men spotted something in the water and rushed to see what it was, thinking it could be a manatee or a dolphin. When they saw the girl in the water, they called nine-one-one, and it didn't take the responding officers from our South District Station long to realize the girl came from the boat they could see out on the water. When they got out there, they found the three others. A pure blood bath, they said. Gonzalez is still throwing up, last thing I heard."

I stared at the photos, my eyes scanning them. "Looks like the harpooned girl died first, so you'll have to assume

25

the killer was standing here, at the stern of the boat," I said and pointed. "Before the girl there ran toward her, probably because they were best friends, maybe still assuming that the harpoon went off by accident. But then the killer pulled a knife and slit her throat. That's why her body is pushed a little further back. The killer was making his way, killing them one after another. The third one, the girl here, was trying to escape before she was harpooned in the leg, as you can see, so she couldn't run anymore. The killer took his time to pull out the harpoon from the first girl and reload; that was why she made it all the way to the edge of the boat before she was stopped. My guess is the fourth one made a jump for it into the water, where the killer probably jumped in after her and pulled her under the water. A guy like him wouldn't risk her surviving to talk. I say you're looking for a diver, someone who knows his way around spearfishing and how to gut a fish. If you look at the way the throat was cut, the incision here and here, it resembles the way you'd cut the head off a fish. But I guess that doesn't narrow it down by much around here, where fishing and diving are common hobbies. Anyway, if you want my take on it, then I'd say he came onto the boat climbing up from the stern side while the kids were hanging out, drinking, and weren't looking in his direction. Once they heard him, the girl here, the first one, rushed to him, probably because it was her father's boat they had borrowed, and she felt responsible. Then she was shot in the heart. This was an assassination. And it was carefully planned."

Fowler folded his hands on the desk and gave me a look, then nodded with a small smile.

"You know I have no way of telling if you're right or not," Fowler said. "Forensics is still working out there, and it'll take a few days before we know these kinds of details."

"I am right, and you know it."

He nodded, chuckling. "You always had a nose for the details. That's why I can't fire you. You're just too darn good of a detective."

That made me smile. Compliments from Fowler were rare.

"So…you want me on the case?" I asked.

## Chapter 9

"NOT SO FAST," Fowler said, shaking his head. "There's more to the story."

"Isn't there always?"

Fowler nodded. "True, but this is more than usual. Do you remember the story of Lucy Lockwood?"

"Sure. It's only been what…a year?" I asked. "She was raped at some school dance, right?"

"She went to prom and, after the party, she went to the beach with her friends, where she claimed a guy raped her while a bunch of kids watched. The guy later called her dad using her phone and told him that his daughter was 'good at sex.' The dad drove down there and found her in the sand all alone. She reported it as a rape and claimed the guy had forced her."

I lifted my eyebrows. "What do you mean *claimed*? I don't understand. You don't believe her?"

"I…well…"

"Who wouldn't believe a seventeen-year-old girl who says she was raped?" I asked, enraged.

"Listen, I know this is a touchy subject since your… your sister was…"

"Raped?" I said. "You can say it out loud, you know. Yes, she was raped when we were teenagers, and now she suffers mental health issues as a result. It's not something anyone would joke around with. And, no, the police didn't believe her either. Told her it was her own fault for dressing the way she did and flirting with the boy who raped her. Don't be like them, Fowler. Don't be like those jerks who told my sister it was her own doing."

Fowler sighed and rubbed his stubble. "Anyway, the investigation back then didn't lead to anything, and a judge dismissed the Lockwood case. There simply was no evidence that she didn't consent; none of the witnesses would say that it wasn't with her consent. They didn't even admit to seeing it happen."

"And the bruises? They didn't tell another story?" I asked.

"You know how it is. You can't argue that it wasn't a part of the act. Witnesses said they saw her flirt with him, act up to him, leading him on at the party."

I shook my head. "You're too much."

Fowler looked down at his papers for a brief second, then back up at me. "The kid had good expensive lawyers who were able to rip the case apart. We did what we could for her, but it just wasn't good enough. Anyway, the thing is, the four girls who turned up dead last night, they are all on the list of witnesses from back then. When Lucy arrived at the hospital, she gave a list of ten names of people who she claimed watched the rape. Last week, another girl, Lisa Turner, turned up dead in a dumpster, also stabbed to death with a fishing knife. They all go to the same high school, and, according to Lucy, they all were on the beach that night when she claims to have been attacked."

I nodded. "And now you're afraid that someone is killing them because of what happened?"

He nodded. "Yes. Morales and his team are talking to the dad today."

"Obviously, but what about the girl? What about Lucy?"

Fowler took off his glasses and wiped sweat from his upper lip. "That's the thing. She went missing eight months ago. Right after the judge dismissed her case, she disappeared. Her parents reported her missing, and we had a search party out and everything, but she was never found. We finally concluded she had run away from home because of what happened. It's not uncommon in cases like these."

I cleared my throat, sending him a suspicious look. "You don't seriously think that Lucy is killing these kids?"

He exhaled. "I don't know what to think, to be honest. But I do know that she has the best motive."

## Chapter 10

"I TAKE it you want me on the case of finding who killed those five girls, right?"

Fowler shook his head. "Wrong. I already have Morales and his team on that one. He investigated the rape back then, and let's be honest, he's here on time and attends all the briefings like he's supposed to."

I stared at my old friend. "You're kidding me, right? You're giving the case to him because he plays by the rules? Murder isn't solved by detectives who play by the rules. You know I'm perfect for this case. You know I'm the only one around here who can solve it."

Fowler shrugged. "You can whine all you want. I need someone I can rely on, someone I trust will pick up the phone when I call. The case is his."

"And what about me? Why did you call me in here if you're not putting me on the case?" I asked.

He leaned back in his chair. His wife and two kids were staring back at him from a picture next to his computer. I knew them all well; we used to be invited over for dinner all the time before Camille got sick. After that, they just stopped asking.

"Well, my first thought was to fire you, but then again, I felt bad because you're the detective with the most solved cases around here, and you're my friend. So, I decided against it."

"Geez, thanks?"

"You're welcome."

"So, what do you have me on?"

He leaned forward and folded his hands on the desk again. "Protection, Harry. I can't have any more kids turn up dead." Fowler pulled out a couple of photos of a young kid no more than seventeen or eighteen. He was wearing the same sly smile in all the pictures like he was keeping some deep secret that he knew he'd get away with. Just looking at him made my skin crawl. It was such a cliché…a white, blue-eyed kid from an affluent suburban area getting away with anything, even rape.

"William Covington was the one Lucy named as her rapist, but who was also later acquitted."

"You've got to be kidding me."

"You say that a lot."

I stared at my old friend, out of words to speak. What the heck was his game? He couldn't be serious about this. He wanted me to be a bloody bodyguard?

"Tell me you're joking. You want me to protect some affluent rapist whose parents' lawyer made sure he could get away with it?"

Fowler nodded. "I don't need to remind you that he was never convicted of any crime, and in the eyes of the law, he is innocent. So, yes, that is what I'm asking of you. If you do your job well, then you might get back to solving cases again soon. If not, then maybe it's time for you to find another line of work more suitable for your needs to come and go as you please."

"You're…"

"Kidding? No, not at all. I suggest you keep this boy alive. Your future depends on it."

## Chapter 11

I DIDN'T STAY at the department. I slammed the door to Fowler's office, then stormed out without even a word to any of my colleagues. I jumped back onto my motorcycle, roared it to life and rode it across town while yelling loudly into the warm Florida wind. I drove out to the beach, then parked the bike and went for a long walk, telling God just how unhappy I was right now with how he was managing my life.

"Don't you see me at all?" I asked, feeling let down. "Between taking care of Camille and Josie, I can't possibly put in the fifty-hour workweek everyone else is. How am I supposed to do this?"

I sat down in the sand, waiting for my answer, but all I could hear in my mind was me telling myself to stop feeling sorry for myself, to pick up myself and continue.

*People need you. Josie needs you more than ever with her teenage years coming up. You can't allow yourself to wallow in self-pity.*

"You can't be pitiful and powerful at the same time," I mumbled, repeating my dad's old mantra. He used to say this to me when I came home from baseball, and we lost or when I got a bad grade, which was pretty often since I wasn't a very strong student and I hated school.

My dad never lost confidence in me, though. He knew I'd amount to something one day. He kept telling me that there was a path for me, one that no one else could walk and that once I found what God's plan for me was, what my talent was, I'd be unstoppable. I thought I had found it when I became a detective. Fowler was right. I had been the one who had solved the most cases in the entire department. Even now, when it had been three years since I had solved anything, I was still ahead of the others. It was my path; it was what I was supposed to do.

Why did I keep running into so much resistance, then?

"Why aren't you making it easier on me if I'm doing what you want?" I asked toward the sky.

I sighed and kept looking at the blue sky above. My dad had been a pastor all my life, and it had seemed so much easier for him. It was like he had this connection with God that I never seemed to be able to find. My dad believed it was because I was still carrying so much anger in me from the time my sister, Reese, was raped when we were teenagers. And he was right about that. I didn't understand why it had to happen and why God didn't protect her. He knew how it was going to ruin her life. Was that his plan for her?

I shook my head. No, I couldn't think like that. I was raised to believe in a good God, and I chose to do so, even with the bad things that happen, even when I didn't understand why Camille had to end up like she did.

My phone vibrated in my pocket, and I looked at the display. It was a text from Fowler. It contained an address and a message:

BE THERE AT 7 AM. BE LATE AND YOU'RE OUT.

I sighed and put the phone back in my pocket, then put my helmet back on.

"If that's how you want to play it, God, then so be it. I'll be a good boy and do as I'm told, but I am not gonna be happy about it. Just saying."

## Chapter 12

SHE HAD WORKED the evening shift and didn't come home until after midnight. Jean felt exhausted as she parked her old Toyota on the street outside of her townhouse. She sighed and looked at her neighbor's house. The lights were out in all the windows.

Jean grabbed her purse, got out, then walked up toward her porch when a sound startled her.

"Hello?"

A face peeked out. It was Harry. He was sitting on the porch swing and waved at her. Jean smiled gently and casually waved back. The sight of him made her heart skip a beat.

"Hi there, neighbor," Harry said.

"Why are you still up?" she asked, even though she knew perfectly well why. Harry hadn't slept much since Camille's overdose.

"Thought I'd enjoy the nice evening outside," he said. "Lots of stars out tonight."

She looked up. "Sure are. How's Camille?"

Jean always felt a pinch in her stomach when

mentioning her name. Camille and Jean had been best friends. They had hung out almost every day, going to lunch, drinking coffee, and yet she had no idea the girl was doing drugs again. It filled her with such a deep sense of guilt every time she thought about it, especially when she saw how much Harry and Josie were struggling. If only she had known. She was a nurse for crying out loud. She knew what to look for. Were there signs she had missed? Anything different in the way Camille acted or spoke? Jean had thought about it over and over again, yet found nothing she could put her finger on.

Camille had been the same in the days leading up to it. Heck, Jean had even spoken to her that same morning before it happened. She had given her those chairs back that she had borrowed for her party a few weeks before. They had a cup of coffee and a couple of donuts that Jean had brought. They talked about Harry and how Camille was worried about his job getting him killed one day, and how tough it was to be the wife of a detective. She feared she might lose him one day, and Josie would have no father. Jean remembered thinking her fear seemed more consuming than usual and wondering if there was a real threat to Harry's life.

Did that drive her back to the drugs? The fear?

No. Camille was happy. She loved her life and her family. It made no sense that she'd suddenly start doing drugs again.

At least not to Jean.

"She's good," Harry said.

Jean could tell he was trying to sound cheerful as usual. He didn't like that she worried.

"She's sleeping," he continued. "I sat by her side all evening after Josie went to bed. I just snuck out half an hour ago. How was your day?"

She shrugged. "Busy as usual when working in the ER. Lots of patients coming down with the flu."

"It is the season," he said with that handsome smile of his. Harry was one big chunk of man, but handsome as the devil. No one could resist that smile of his, least of all, Jean.

But it could never be them. Not in a million years. He was still married, and Jean was Camille's best friend.

It could never happen. Ever.

"Anyway, I should…" She pointed at her house with her thumb.

"Yeah, me too," he said. "I have work to do early in the morning, at seven a.m. New assignment from the boss. My dad will be over to eat breakfast with Josie and make sure she gets to school on time."

"Then, as your nurse, I'll recommend you hit the sack," she said with a chuckle.

Keys in her hand and purse slung over her shoulder, she walked up to the steps leading to her house, sensing how his stare followed her every move. As she was about to walk up, she turned to look at him, then smiled.

"I'll take care of Camille tomorrow morning. You just worry about your big case or whatever it is you're doing."

He exhaled. "I hoped you'd say that. You're a lifesaver, Jean."

She nodded. It didn't feel like much, not since she was unable to save her own best friend's life.

"Goodnight," Harry said.

She reached her door, then sent him one last glance. He had already left the porch and was walking inside the house as she whispered with longing in her voice:

"Goodnight, Harry Handsome."

## Chapter 13

I DROVE up the long driveway to the mansion situated on five acres of oceanfront land and walked up to the front entrance at precisely seven a.m. I wasn't going to give Fowler the pleasure of firing me for being late. While waiting for someone to open the front door of the Spanish mansion, I took a quick glance around me and saw the tennis court located in the corner of the lot.

As the wooden door slid open, I showed the woman behind the door my badge. "Detective Hunter, Miami PD. I believe I am expected."

The small—very beautiful—woman mumbled something in a foreign language, then showed me inside, where a tall blonde woman in a tan dress greeted me.

"Mrs. Covington?" I said. "I'm Detective Hunter from Miami PD. I'm here for the protection of your son."

The woman nodded. She seemed like she was in distress. "Yes, yes, of course," she said. "Please, come on in."

"I just need to know a little more about William's

schedule this week," I said, "so I can make sure to keep him safe."

She gave me a half-smile. "He has school from nine to three-thirty every day. He has tennis lessons here at the house on Tuesdays and Thursdays from four till six. His teacher comes here to train him. On the weekends, he usually goes golfing or boating with his friends. He also practices his violin on Wednesdays with a private teacher. She comes here."

I was writing notes on my notepad. "So, he basically only leaves the house to go to school and on the weekends?"

"Yes."

I nodded. That sounded like a pretty easy task. She gave me a look. "So, is there...is there anything we need to do? I understand that you believe there's a threat to him? Do we need to keep him home while this is going on?"

I exhaled and ran a hand through my hair. "I think you should just go on the way you usually do. We don't really know exactly what is going on, or whether your son is in danger or not, but we do know that several other kids from his school were killed, and they were all witnesses in the Lockwood case."

Mrs. Covington's lips tightened. "Oh...that. Awful story. I'm glad the judge realized my boy had nothing to do with it."

I stared at her, scrutinizing her, then realized she fully believed in her son's innocence. Of course, she did. She was his mother. She had to believe it, right? How else could you go on after something like that? How would you ever be able to look your son in the eyes again, knowing he had raped someone?

Mrs. Covington's face lit up as someone approached us, coming down the stairs. I recognized him from the pictures in Fowler's office. He hadn't changed much since they were taken. His light brown hair fell into his face as he walked, and he ran a hand through it to move it.

"William," his mother said as she grabbed his arm and pulled him toward me. The boy let her, probably because I was there, then removed his arm from her grip.

"Meet Detective Hunter from Miami PD," she said. "He'll be protecting you over the next few days, you know...like we discussed. After what happened to..."

The mother received a look from her son, and she stopped talking. William reached out his hand and looked into my eyes while shaking my hand.

"Detective Hunter, nice to meet you."

Shaking his hand made my skin crawl, thinking about how those same hands had touched and abused Lucy Lockwood. I was towering above him with my six-foot-eight to his five-foot-eleven. I kept thinking about Reese and how her rapist had gotten away with it, too, how she had to go to school and see him every day, laughing at her. The thought made me want to beat this kid up right here and now.

"We're glad you're here, Detective," Mrs. Covington said. "It's an awful ordeal with what happened to those kids. William knows them from school and...well..."

"Mom," William said, annoyed. "I'm capable of taking care of myself. I barely knew those kids."

"But William, if there's a killer...if that girl is out there killing..."

He gave her a look. "Mom, stop it, will you? You're being paranoid. I can easily handle some girl."

"But...but William..."

"Stop it, Mom."

William hissed the last part at his mother.

"Anyway," I said, feeling uncomfortable. It felt like I

42

had landed in the middle of something I had no desire to become a part of. "I'm just going to be parked out on the street, so if you see anything or hear anything, then…" I handed her my card. "My cell phone number is here, or you can just come out to talk to me. I'll be staying close to William all day, and I'll wait outside of his school as well."

Mrs. Covington walked me to the door and held it for me. "Thank you, Detective. We appreciate it immensely."

I stopped as I reached the door. "Where is Mr. Covington?"

"He…he's not here."

I stared at her as her eyes avoided mine. "As in he doesn't live here anymore?"

She lifted her eyes, and they met mine. "Yes. He moved out. We're separated."

"I am sorry to hear that."

"Don't be," William said from behind her. Mrs. Covington turned to give him a look. William sent her a sly smile, the very same one I recognized from the photos.

"Don't mind him," she said, addressed to me. "He's angry at us for separating. He blames his father."

"Are there any siblings, or is William your only child?" I asked. "For safety reasons, I need to know how many people are in the household."

She shook her head. "No. There's just William and me here. And Dalisay, of course, the woman who let you in. She takes care of us."

## Chapter 14

WHEN SHE TOLD people her name was Sophia, they usually assumed it was because of her Spanish heritage, because of her brown skin, but it wasn't. Sophia was half Jamaican and half German. Her parents had both worked on a cruise ship and ended up loving Miami so much— especially because of the melting pot of diversity that it has —they finally settled there and became naturalized. Today, her dad had his own tech company while her mother ran a rather successful investment company. She was one of the only moms in Sophia's friend group who worked, and that made Sophia proud. She, too, was going to make something of herself one day.

At least that was what she had always told herself while growing up. Now, as she was sitting in class, staring at William Covington's neck in front of her, she wasn't sure she'd even make it that far.

Four of the seats in her math class were empty—four seats where Georgiana, Katelyn, Sandra, and Martina usually sat. Sophia couldn't stop staring at the empty chairs, feeling the chill run down her spine.

*Murdered,* they had said on TV. *Brutally assassinated.*

The thought made the hairs on Sophia's neck stand up. She, too, was supposed to have gone with her friends on that boat that night, only she had decided not to at the last minute because she had to get up early the next day.

There was a fifth victim; they had also said on TV. Lisa Turner. She had been found the week before in a dumpster, stabbed to death. Back then, they had all believed she had met her killer coincidentally...that she was walking the streets when she met her attacker, that it was some drug addict or maybe a crazy homeless person. It had been terrible, yes, awful, of course, but at least it didn't mean anyone else was in danger. With the four others gone too, that had all changed. She couldn't help feeling this killer was making his way through her entire friend group. It didn't seem possible that it was a coincidence anymore.

*And you know perfectly well why, don't you?*

Sophia trembled again and looked away from the empty chairs, then shook her head. She almost didn't come to school this morning, but then realized it was no use. She had to go on as usual, even though she was beyond terrified.

The police had sent someone to her house and spoken to her parents. They had told them to make sure Sophia was at home from nine p.m. until six a.m. They were also going to have a patrol car drive up and down the street several times a day and have one outside of the school. That made her ease up slightly, but it didn't really make her feel comfortable. Somehow, she had a feeling this killer would get to her, no matter how many police surrounded her.

It was only a matter of time.

The bell rang, and Sophia gathered her things, then

grabbed her backpack, hurrying out of the classroom before William could talk to her.

"Sophia," his voice sounded behind her.

She stopped in her tracks and closed her eyes briefly. She had hoped to avoid this.

Sophia turned to look at him as he approached her, books under his arm. He was so devilishly handsome; it was unbearable.

"Did the police come to your house?" he asked.

She looked around to make sure no one could listen in on their conversation, then nodded.

"Yes. And you?"

"They're guarding me all day. Some burned-out detective who doesn't even try to hide that he'd rather see me dead and couldn't care less. He looked like a drunk with a big shiner and everything."

"It's awful…what happened to the others."

"I think it's Lucy," he said.

Sophia stared at him with her eyes wide. Thinking about Lucy didn't make her feel good. William shrugged as they walked into the hallway toward their next class.

"I think she might be crazy enough, don't you?" he continued.

"I don't…know."

"She's been gone for eight months now," he said.

"So, you're thinking she's back with a vengeance?"

William smiled nervously. "Something like that. She didn't get what she wanted in the first place when the judge denied her case. But she's not done yet. This could be her next step."

Sophia stopped at her locker and looked up at William and into his deep blue eyes. He smiled gently, then placed his hands on both of her upper arms, his glare piercing into her eyes. It made her feel uncomfortable, but she couldn't pull away. He was holding her too tightly.

"We can't let her win. Do you hear me?"

He spat the words out, hissing at her angrily. She shook her head while his hands were hurting her arms, and she was squirming in pain.

"Of course not, William, of course not."

He kept staring into her eyes while crushing her arms with his touch until tears sprang to her eyes. His nostrils were flaring like he was almost enjoying it when finally, his smile returned, and he eased up on her.

"Good," he said and let go. He ran a hand through his hair and exhaled, satisfied. He grabbed her chin and lifted her face upward to make sure he had her full attention. Looking into his eyes made her sick to her stomach.

"We agree, then. We've got to stick together in this."

"Of course," she said, feeling her sore arms. As he turned around on his heel and left, she ran to the bathroom and into a stall where she closed the door. She rolled up the sleeves on her shirt and looked at the huge purple bruises he had left there where his hands had held her tight. She sat down on the toilet, hid her face between her hands, and began to cry, shaking her head.

"What have I done? What have I done?"

## Chapter 15

I SPENT the day in one of the police department's mini-vans that we used for stakeouts. It was equipped with a computer that was hooked up to our system back at the station, so it was possible to work while spending hours and hours staking someone out.

I spent my time doing a little research. I knew it wasn't my case, but it couldn't hurt anything to take a look, could it?

Fact was, I couldn't stop thinking about this girl, Lucy Lockwood, the girl that had been raped and the one Fowler believed might be killing her old friends. I kept thinking about my sister, then wondering, if that had been her, would she have been able to kill because of what happened to her?

Maybe.

I, for one, wanted to kill the guy back then. I did track him down and beat him up on the street of his neighborhood a few weeks after it happened—nothing serious, just enough for him to feel it for a couple of weeks afterward and be reminded that I was watching him. But killing him? And the people who had witnessed it?

It was hard to tell. The motive was there; I'd give Fowler that much. But in my book, it sounded more like something her father might attempt.

Had they had a chance to talk to him yet?

I opened the case file and read through parts of it, skipping the pictures from the boat since I had seen them thoroughly, and I had a pretty good photographic memory, which wasn't always a good thing, especially not when seeing stuff like that. I couldn't get the pictures out of my mind again once they got in there. They could haunt me for months…maybe even years.

I read the father's statement that Morales and his team had taken the day before. Mr. Lockwood had been out of town all weekend, on a business trip and had all the evidence they needed, including an itinerary and hotel receipts. When asked about the group of teenagers, if he knew any of them, he said that, yes, he knew they were all witnesses to what happened to his daughter, and that it was a terrible thing that they had died. Especially for him. He was still working with the DA to get them to reopen the case, and now his list of possible witnesses was dwindling. He had no interest in seeing them dead. It made no sense for him to kill any of them.

He made a good point, I decided. If there was anyone he wanted dead, it was the boy. Why was William still alive?

I shook my head, feeling a little confused when I received a text from Josie.

I GOT A 98 ON MY MATH TEST.

The message was followed by a sad face, telling me she had hoped for more. I chuckled at my overachieving daughter and texted her back.

GOOD JOB, SWEETIE.

I WANTED 100 THO. I MADE ONE MISTAKE. ONE.

98 IS PERFECTLY FINE, I wrote back.

I couldn't help laughing at my daughter, yet hoping she'd never have bigger problems than that.

I bit my lip when thinking about how hard she pushed herself and that she had done so ever since her mother got sick. She had always done well in school before that, but when her mother overdosed, she took it to a new level. Was she trying to prove something? Was she trying to distance herself from the life her mother had?

Whatever it was, I just prayed that she wouldn't burn out.

I returned to the computer, then read through some more testimonies while the hours passed in front of the school. I opened the latest autopsy report that had come in just an hour earlier and looked through it. Then, I stopped. I reread something again and again, while images and sentences rushed through my mind.

I grabbed my phone and called the Medical Examiner's Office and my old friend Emilia Lopez.

## Chapter 16

"WELL, hello there, stranger, long time no see. What's it been, two years?" Emilia said as she picked up the phone.

I exhaled when hearing her voice. It brought back a lot of memories. Emilia had always been a close colleague of mine, always ready to help me with my cases and push me ahead in the line when I needed it. It had been a while, yes, because I hadn't been involved in much detective work over the past couple of years.

"What can I help you with?"

"You found a chess piece on the boat?" I asked.

"Well, I didn't; the techs at the scene did," Emilia said. "But, yes. They found a black rook on the deck of the boat. I didn't know it was your case? I thought Morales and his team had it?"

I cleared my throat and didn't answer. "But there was a chess piece in the pocket of the girl found in the dumpster too, right?"

Emilia exhaled. "Yes, a pawn. We found no fingerprints or any DNA on either of them, though."

"What about the one from the boat. Did you find any trace of neoprene from a wet suit?"

"Yes, as a matter of fact, we did."

I leaned back my head in the car, leaning it against the neck rest while pondering over this. It fit well with my theory that the killer came from the ocean. If the killer had been a diver, swimming to the boat like it was my theory, he'd be wearing a wetsuit. At this time of year, he'd have to. The ocean was warm in Florida, but this was January. This was still puzzling me. Did he come by his own boat? The boat with the girls was too far out for someone just to swim there.

"The killer leaves these chess pieces, but why?" I asked. It wasn't really for her as much as it was for me.

Was there a message to it? It had to have some significance, something this killer was trying to tell us.

Emilia chuckled. "That's your department, Detective."

"Of course. Thanks for the update; I'll leave you to your work."

"How's Camille," she said as I was about to hang up. "And Josie? How's she holding up?"

"She's okay, I think. Hanging in there. Camille is the same."

"I'm so sorry to hear that, Harry," Emilia said. "You know how I loved Camille."

"We all did," I said with an exhale. "We all did."

"Well, it's good to have you back, Hunter," Emilia said. "We missed you; well, I did. I missed you."

I hung up and stared at the display on my phone of an old photo of Camille and Josie that I used as a background. It was taken four years ago on our trip to New York...the last trip we had taken together as a family. I touched her face gently with my finger, letting it run down her smooth features. It hurt to know she would never look at me the way she did in this picture again. I would never get to see her with the love in her eyes that was so familiar.

*I miss being the one you love.*

I stared at my one true love, missing her, then couldn't stop thinking about Lucy Lockwood. I lifted my glance and looked into the street, then realized I didn't buy into the theory that Lucy had come back to kill everyone involved in her rape. But if she wasn't the killer, then it opened up a whole other can of worms. She could be another victim. Or she could be in hiding because she knew who the killer was.

No matter what, I had to find her, fast, before any more kids turned up dead.

I looked at the school in front of me, then started up the minivan. I knew I was supposed to stay and watch William Covington. But there were still four hours till school was out. That left me plenty of time to get back here in time for when the bell rang.

No one would even notice I had been gone.

## Chapter 17

VALENTINA LOCKWOOD'S hands were shaking as she served me coffee. She was a stunning woman in her mid-thirties, originally from Colombia, she told me.

"The detective isn't interested in knowing where you're from," her husband, Robert Lockwood, snapped.

Valentina gave him a look, then shook her head.

"No, of course not. I don't know why I said that."

"Anything might turn out to be useful," I said, addressed to her. "Let me be the judge of what is important and what is not."

"What is this regarding?" Robert Lockwood asked. "I had a couple of your colleagues here yesterday and told them I was out of town when those kids were killed. I had just gotten back. Why are you here again?"

I sipped the coffee. It tasted heavenly.

"This is really good coffee," I said.

Valentina smiled nervously. "Colombian. My mother sends the beans every now and then, whenever she can make it to the post office. Her legs aren't what they used to be."

I smiled, turning up the charm to make her feel better about herself and comfortable in my presence. She was obviously broken.

"Well, it's the best coffee I've had in a very long time; thank you for that."

Mr. Lockwood put his cup down hard, causing my cup to jump. "Why are you here? Could we get to the point? I have a busy schedule, and I already told you people everything I know."

"I'm sorry," I said. "I just…well, when I smelled that coffee, I had to ask for a cup. No, I'm not here to talk about the teenagers on the boat. I'm here because I want to find your daughter."

Mrs. Lockwood's eyes grew wide. "Find her…but I thought you stopped the search; it has been so long?"

I exhaled and nodded. "I know. I know. It has been a long time. But she is still a missing teenager and…"

"They think she's killing them," Robert Lockwood said with a snort. "That's the only reason he's here."

Valentina wrinkled her forehead. "They do what?"

"They think Lucy is back and that she's killing the kids from that night because she didn't get that Covington boy to pay for…what he did. Because they wouldn't speak up against him."

"What? I don't understand?" Valentina said. "They think…you think that my daughter…is…is…"

"Of course, they do," Robert continued. "They think either I did it or she did. It's pretty obvious…as revenge."

"I don't," I said, swallowing yet another sip of that delicious warm substance that made my taste buds dance.

"Excuse me?" Robert said.

"I said, I don't. I can't talk for my police department, but I can tell you that I don't believe your daughter is killing anyone. Why would she kill those people who are her only witnesses to the crime committed against her?"

Robert stared at me, surprised.

"I want to find your daughter, so we can prove that it wasn't her. But I am going to need your help."

The two of them looked at one another. Tears sprang to Valentina's eyes. She reached over to grab her husband's hand.

"You'll have to excuse us," Robert said, "if we find this a little hard to believe…that you are here to help. We've been met only with suspicion from the police department ever since we found our daughter…in the sand, beaten and…"

"Raped," I said, swallowing a knot growing in my throat, remembering how hard it was for my parents to say the word when it was Reese, how deeply it destroyed their faith in the justice system and the world. That was the only time I found my dad on the verge of losing his faith in God.

He nodded, his eyes avoiding mine as they grew red-rimmed. "Yes, that. They never seemed to believe her story. They kept telling her she had been flirting with the boy, that they believed she wanted it to happen, but then she regretted it afterward when thinking about what her parents might say when they found out. They even had the audacity to tell her that she dressed provocatively and sexy to lure him in. No matter how much we protested, they kept on and on about how she had made the whole thing up, that they couldn't find any evidence that she was raped. What about the bruises? I asked them. Still, the judge dismissed it because none of the witnesses dared to stand up for our Lucy. They are terrified of the kid, you know? That's why."

"They're terrified of William Covington?" I asked.

Robert nodded and looked away for a brief second, then wiped his eyes with the palms of his hands.

"It's true," Valentina added. "All the kids are scared of him. He's been bullying them since middle school. No one ever dares to say anything. Lucy told me about him before. He once even made some guy burn himself with cigarettes all over his face, threatening to reveal to the rest of the school that he was gay. In middle school, he cut off a girl's hair and shaved her head in the bathroom because she had told on him to the dean, telling him that William vaped in the bathroom. He never got in trouble, though, because he threatened the dean that if he told his parents, he'd reveal that the dean had an affair with one of the teachers. All the teachers are terrified of him too. No one will ever dare to stand up to him."

I wrote it all down on my notepad while thinking about the look William had given his mother at the house. She, too, seemed nervous around him, and slightly anxious.

"Mr. and Mrs. Lockwood," I said and lifted my eyes to look first him in the eyes, then her. "I need you to be completely honest with me. Do you have any idea where Lucy might be?"

They both shook their heads.

"We don't," she said. "We haven't seen her since August fourteenth. She was at home when the call came from our lawyer. The judge had dismissed the case, he said. We sat down and talked to her about it. She ran to her room, and we let her stay up there for a few hours, crying it out while discussing what we wanted to do next. Robert said he'd appeal the decision and try to get the DA to reopen the case. We even talked about moving away. For months, she had to go to school every day and see her rapist there, laughing in her face, tormenting her while she could do nothing. We talked about signing her up for a boarding school to get her out of here, but we didn't want him to win, you know? We wanted to see him behind bars where he belongs for everything he's done, all the people he has tormented."

Valentina stopped and wiped her nose on a napkin. Her husband took over.

"When we went up to her room later that night, she wasn't there. Her bag was gone, and so were some of her clothes. We realized she had run away, but still hoped and prayed she'd come back soon."

"Did she have any money? A phone?"

"She had taken some cash from my drawer," Valentina said. "But it can't have been more than maybe a thousand dollars."

"A teenager can get pretty far for less," I said. "Does she have any relatives she might have gone to see? Or old friends?"

"They're all around here, and we've called each and every one," Robert said. "I can give you the list we gave the police back then."

"Yes, please, and her phone? Did she take it?"

"She left her phone here," Robert said. "In her room."

"Can I see it?" I asked.

"They already went through it when we reported her missing," he said. "They went through all her stuff, but found nothing."

I nodded. "I know, but it never hurts to take a second look. Also, if she had a computer, I'd like to take a look at that as well, if you don't mind."

Valentina nodded at her husband, and he disappeared upstairs while I finished my coffee. Robert came back with an iPhone in his hand and a laptop under his arm. He handed me both.

"I'll have both things back to you as soon as I'm done with them," I said.

"Please," Valentina said and grabbed my hands between hers. "Please, take your time with it. Just help us find our girl. She's a good girl; you must know this, Detective. She truly is; she does volunteer work at the animal shelter, she gets straight A's, she's compassionate toward her friends and would go through fire for them. She would never hurt anyone, never. She must be so scared right now. Please, just find her."

I nodded, looking at them both. I knew better than to promise them anything, yet I really wanted to. If this had been my Josie, I don't know what I would have done. First, the rape and then this? It was almost too much for one family to take.

"I will do everything in my power," I said. "I can promise you that much."

## Chapter 18

A WEARY MAN with a cigarette dangling from his lips answered the door of the second-floor apartment. I was back in Overtown and knew the eyes staring back at me a little better than I was proud of.

"Shoot," the guy said, trying to close the door in my face. I put my foot in it to block it, then pushed the door open so brutally it knocked into the guy's face.

"Ouch!" he yelled and stumbled backward.

I walked inside and closed the door behind me. The guy was known as T-Bone because his body resembled one.

"I haven't done anything," T-Bone said, touching his nose and wiping away the blood. "I've been a good boy."

"I'm sure you have," I said and picked him up from the floor, then dragged him to his ripped leather couch. I sat in a recliner next to it, then handed him a tissue to wipe the blood away.

"I'm serious," he said. "I stayed out of trouble like you told me to. No drugs. You can search the entire place; you won't find any."

"I'm not here for that," I said. "I need your help with something."

T-Bone's face lit up. "Oh, really? You need my help now, do ya? How the tables have turned, huh? What's in it for me?"

"Honor and glory," I said and slapped him over the head. "What do you mean, what's in it for me?"

He made the international sign for money, and I exhaled, knowing it would come. "There'll be a reward," I said. I had talked about this with the Lockwoods when leaving, and they had agreed to pay one if it led to finding their daughter. "It could be quite substantial, actually. The girl I need you to find for me has some very wealthy parents."

That did the trick. I could see the change in T-Bone's eyes. Money always did the trick. It was disgusting. But I needed this guy. He knew every corner of town and every face of the criminal world. He knew what pedophiles lived under which bridge and what mobsters to stay clear of if you wanted to keep living. If the girl were living on the streets, he'd know or be able to find out.

I grabbed my phone and found a picture of her. "This girl. Have you seen her?"

He looked at the picture, then sniffled. "Pretty girl. Wouldn't last long on the streets, though." He handed me back the phone. "Haven't seen her, I'm afraid. But send me the pic and I'll see what I can find. I know the guys down by the port would love to get their hands on a girl like that."

I exhaled, knowing he was talking about the human traffickers. Trafficking was a huge problem in my town and a multimillion-dollar business. Six times last year, smugglers had been caught when trying to bring in girls through the port illegally, and we only saw the tip of the iceberg.

Thirty-six arrests had been made last year, but there were more and more traffickers coming too, knowing there was a lot more money being made in trafficking than most other crimes these days. If they had gotten their nasty hands on Lucy, she could be anywhere in the country by now.

I sent him the picture and waited for him to receive it.

"I'll ask around," he said, lighting up another cigarette. "But it better be worth it."

"That's all I'm asking."

## Chapter 19

I DROVE THROUGH TOWN, frequenting several of my other informers, spreading the word about Lucy Lockwood and hoping to get some information or at least one sighting of her, but I had no such luck. I also visited her best friend's house and talked to her mother, then visited the shelter where she volunteered and asked around to see if anyone was close to Lucy or might know anything about where she might be hiding. So far, all I got were positive statements when asking about her. Lucy was a well-liked girl, and everyone that knew her kept referring to her as one of the good girls. The same went for all five of the girls that had been murdered. They were straight-A students, members of the Bible club, debate club, or chorus, all taking part in the community, all doing volunteer work outside of school, and being just plain good girls.

I drove to South Beach and into an alley where I parked and took the back entrance into a building. I ran the three stories up and knocked on the door to an apartment.

A woman opened the door, her dreadlocks pulled back

and held by a hair tie. She was wearing baggy harem pants and a small crop top.

"Hunter? What brings you here?"

"Can I come in?"

She looked like she had to think it over for a few seconds, then agreed. Her name was Alvita or The Plague, as they called her in the cyber world. I just called her Al. Al was a former CIA hacker who had turned her back on the world after seeing what it was capable of. Now, she hid in this small apartment where no one would find her. Except for me, that was since I had known her for years and used her to do the things our own IT department couldn't do fast enough or weren't skilled enough to do.

"What's up?"

"I need your help," I said.

"I kind of figured that," she said with a grin.

I handed her the computer and the phone. "Techs have been through it all, but I need you to dig deeper, do your magic. This girl is missing, and she needs to be found, asap. Can you do that for me?"

She shrugged and placed the computer on the desk. "Give me the rest of the day. I'll be in touch."

I left her apartment, then ran down the stairs when realizing how late it was. I only had half an hour to get back to the school in time. It was a fifteen-minute drive if there was no traffic, which only happened in my dreams. I jumped into the minivan, closed the door, and stepped on the accelerator, pulling into the street. I hadn't made it far when I spotted a black car coming up behind me. I hadn't noticed it before, but now that it was getting so close, I suddenly saw it very clearly.

"What the heck?" I mumbled. The black Hyundai drove very close to me, pressuring me to drive faster.

"Go around me if you're in such a hurry, you idiot," I

yelled at the rearview mirror. The windows on the black Hyundai were tinted, so I couldn't see a face behind the windshield.

Finally, it drove up on my side, accelerating till it was right next to me. I tried to see the driver but couldn't see a face. Then, as I expected it to drive past me, it turned toward me instead, making a sudden move sideways, slamming into my van's front end, causing my minivan to drive off the road. I bumped into the grass but managed to regain control of it just when the Hyundai took up the chase and drove into the side of my van, forcing me to run into the guardrail. As my minivan came to a sudden halt, I flew forward and hit my head hard on the steering wheel.

## Chapter 20

I MUST HAVE BEEN out for a few minutes because once I came to, the Hyundai was long gone. I was all alone on the side of the road, my head pounding like crazy.

What the heck was that? Who was that?

*Someone sending you a message.*

I swallowed, trying to think straight, blinking my eyes to better focus, and looked at my phone. I was more than late now. There was no way I'd be able to make it back to the school in time. I looked at my bruise in the mirror. My forehead was slowly turning purple. My face wasn't a pretty sight.

*Jean's gonna yell at me.*

I turned the key and was happy to realize that the minivan could start again. The front was pushed in, and the sides severely dented. It made a loud rattling sound that couldn't be healthy when I drove it, but other than that, it was fine. It could still take me places, and that was good enough for me. I didn't even want to try and think about what to tell them at the station once I handed it back. How was I going to explain this to Fowler? Well, I didn't have to worry about that yet. I had the minivan for the time I needed it to protect William. Then I'd make up some story if I had to.

I drove carefully, staying just above the speed limit, then reached the school and stopped the minivan outside. I looked at my watch and realized the bell had rung at least fifteen minutes ago.

"Shoot," I said and looked around to see if I could spot William. Most of the kids had already left, and William's Land Rover wasn't in the spot it had been when we arrived this morning. He had already left.

I shrugged, then drove back to his parents' house and parked on the street outside. I exhaled, then looked at my forehead again and cursed the long-gone Hyundai. If only I had seen the face of the driver or seen the license plate when it took off. But I didn't. I had no way of identifying the car.

I opened my phone and tapped on it, checking my emails, then received a text from Josie, who had come home from school. It was our deal that she texted me as soon as she got back, so I knew she was home and safe. I wasn't really calm till I received those words from her:

HOME.

I answered with a thumbs up. She texted me back.

MOM'S ASLEEP. JEAN IS HERE. SHE FED HER BEFORE SHE FELL ASLEEP. SHE'S COOKING FOR US TONIGHT.

I felt my mouth water. Jean was an excellent cook. She was probably working the night shift tonight, which was my luck. I was already looking forward to it. Fowler had told me I only had to stay at the house till six. After that, he'd have a couple of patrols drive by the street at night. The Covingtons' house had security alarms and cameras, so they'd know if anyone tried to break in.

I, for one, couldn't wait to call it a day.

Once I had been out there for about an hour, the gate opened, and Mrs. Covington stepped out, tapping along on her black high heels. She approached me, looking distressed. I rolled down the window as I realized she was there to talk to me.

"What's wrong?" I asked.

"Where's William?"

My eyes grew wide.

"He's not at the house?"

She shook her head. "No. He never came home from school. I thought you were keeping an eye on him; wasn't that what you were supposed to do?"

I swallowed, feeling an outbreak of cold sweat all over my body. This wasn't good. Fowler would kill me if he found out. No, worse than that, he'd fire me, and then how would I pay the bills?

"He might have gone to the country club for a round of golf or just be hanging out at the restaurant with his friends," she said. "He used to do that a lot. Maybe he's with his friend, Krueger. I'll text you his address and number."

"Okay. I'll go look for him," I said and started up the coughing minivan.

# Chapter 21

OF COURSE, the boy was nowhere near the country club, nor was he with this Krueger fellow, and his friend hadn't seen him since sixth period, he said. I should have known it wasn't going to be that easy. I felt like an idiot for driving across town looking for this boy, this eighteen-year-old kid who probably was just hanging out with his friends somewhere, maybe picking up girls. I felt ridiculous like I had suddenly become a babysitter for some affluent wealthy kid, who, by the way, had raped a girl and gotten away with it.

But it was my job right now, and I had to stick with it. I simply had to.

"Come on, William; where are you?" I mumbled as I drove up the street back toward the school. I kept calling the boy's cell, but he wasn't answering. After the twelfth try, I threw my phone on the seat next to me, growling. As I drove past a house next to the school, I suddenly spotted William's Land Rover in the driveway. I hit the brakes so hard I almost hit my head a second time when the minivan stopped abruptly.

I panted agitatedly, then looked out the window and spotted William standing in the driveway, talking to someone. The two of them were obviously in some sort of dispute. The guy was older, an adult. I stayed in my van for a little longer, observing them. William was approaching the guy, and it was very easy to tell that the guy was terrified of him. William had that grin on his face, that sly smile. He reached out toward the guy like he wanted to caress his face when instead, he smacked him across the face. The guy fell backward, as surprised as I was.

"What the heck?"

William was holding something in his hand, and as I opened the car door and was about to jump out, I heard him tell the guy to pull up his shirt. The guy did it, and William, grinning, placed a stun gun on the man's skin. The man screamed in pain as the gun sent waves of shock through his body.

"HEY!" I yelled and began running up the driveway. But as I did, William didn't even look at me. I could hear the sound of the stun gun electrical charge against the man's skin.

"STOP, you bastard!" I yelled and felt for the gun in my holster, taking the grip in my hand, ready to pull it should it be necessary. "What do you think you're doing?"

As he heard me yell, he turned his head to look at me, still continuing to stun the man, then he laughed.

I pulled out my gun. "William, stop that right now!"

William didn't move. He stared at me, still holding the stun gun in his hand, still laughing at me like he enjoyed it even more with me watching him.

"William! Step away from that man right now."

He pulled the gun away, then looked at the man once more, lifting his fist, pretending like he was going to hit him before finally pulling away.

"If it isn't Detective Hunter," he said, walking toward me, the look of a madman in his eyes.

"Stop right there," I said.

That made him laugh again. "Or what? You'll shoot?"

"If I have to."

He kept walking toward me, smiling widely. "But you'd never do that, would you, Detective? Because you are here to protect me. That's your job; isn't it?"

"Not when you're hurting people, William. I'll have to take you in…"

"For what? Mr. James here doesn't want any trouble; do you?"

The man shook his head without looking at either of us. "N-no, sir. No trouble."

"See? No witness, no accusations, no case. You're wasting everyone's time here, Detective."

"I saw you do it."

"So? If the victim won't say anything, I hardly think you have a case. Besides, we wouldn't want your boss to know that you weren't where you were supposed to be today; would we? It wouldn't be much fun if he found out that you left your post; would it?"

My hand was wrapped tight around the grip of the gun, my knuckles turning white. I wanted to hurt him so badly. My pulse was sky high, and my hand holding the gun was shaking with anger.

William smiled and walked up to me, then placed a hand on my shoulder. "I didn't think so."

## Chapter 22

"I'M TELLING YOU, Jean, it's hard to protect a kid when you want to strangle him yourself."

I grabbed the spoon and served myself a second round of spaghetti and meatballs. Jean made the best food in the world...the smell alone was heavenly.

"Why do you have to protect him?" Josie asked.

I shrugged. "It's my job."

"I thought you were a detective," Josie said.

I exhaled. "I thought so too."

"Sometimes, you have to do stuff you don't really want to," Jean said. "Just like at my job. There's a lot of stuff I don't enjoy doing, but I have to. I bet there's also a lot of homework you don't want to do."

Josie nodded, then rose to her feet with her plate between her hands. "Speaking of, I have homework to do."

She gave me a kiss, then rushed up the stairs. My dad had come over to eat too. Jean had invited him over as she usually did when cooking for us, and now he left the table and walked to the living room, where he sat in a recliner and turned on the TV. He closed his eyes briefly and grunted with satisfaction. He had gotten old over the past few years since my mom died last year. Seeing him alone broke my heart. Those two had been inseparable.

Jean smiled and leaned over the table while I finished my plate. I had told her everything about the case and William when I got back while she was still in the kitchen, cooking. I had to. She took one look at my forehead and demanded to know what I had been up to.

"I just hope I can find Lucy," I said with a sigh. I patted my very full stomach. "I fear she might be in trouble. I don't like that she has been missing for this long."

"I'm sure her parents are completely devastated," Jean said. "I can't imagine going through first her being raped and then…"

I nodded. "It makes me so mad to think about that poor girl being dragged through all the suspicion when she reported the rape to the police. It makes me want to yell at my colleagues. What the heck are they thinking, telling her she is at fault? Who does that? And now this guy is just running around, harassing people and acting like a bully. I can't believe they're having me protect that bastard. You should have seen him today, Jean. I swear; he did this to me on purpose. To get rid of me, get me off his back. He saw I was gone and then knew he could use it. He is that calculated."

Jean gave me a look. "Really? Do you think he might have killed those kids on the boat?"

I exhaled and leaned back. "I don't know, but he sure fits the profile a lot better than Lucy. Everyone I talk to praises her for being such a sweet young girl, always helpful, taking care of others."

"Could William be getting rid of them because of what they saw? Is that your theory? But they already told the police they didn't see anything, and you said that was because they were terrified of him."

"Maybe they threatened to tell; maybe they changed their minds," I said. "That's my theory."

"Or maybe they have something else on him that he doesn't want them to tell anyone," Jean said.

Josie came down the stairs with a deep exhale and placed a book on the table. "I don't know how to do this."

"What is it, sweetie?" I said, surprised. Josie usually had no trouble with any of her homework.

"I need to do this project for Spanish, but I don't know how to do it."

"Let me have a look at it," Jean said. "I'm pretty good at Spanish."

Jean got up and walked with Josie back up to her room. I grabbed the plates and started to clean up. As I passed my dad in the recliner, he opened his eyes.

"When are you going to do something about it?"

I wrinkled my forehead. "About what?"

He nodded toward the stairs. "About her?"

"Jean? What on earth are you talking about? In case you missed it, I'm still married, Dad."

"She's here every day, son."

"Because she helps out, taking care of Camille," I said, getting annoyed with him. "Besides, I don't think she ever thinks about me in that way. I'm her best friend's husband."

"Open your eyes, son. She takes care of you and Josie, doing homework with her. What woman does that?"

I answered with a growl.

"You know what? I have a wife. I don't need another woman in my life, and besides, it's none of your business."

# Chapter 23

I STARED at the one-story gray building, which held about a thousand teenagers, while eating the sandwich that Jean had made for me when she came over earlier. I had spent the morning hours, while the sun rose outside our window, talking to Camille, telling her everything about the case. Jean had said she'd make sure to change the feeding tube and wash Camille, while I had to rush out of the door.

And now I was sitting here with nothing to do with myself, but ready, just in case. Using the computer in the beat-up minivan, I did a little research, looking at chess pieces and their meanings. I also looked through the case files from the boat to see if anything new had come in…if Morales and his team had any breakthroughs, but nothing had changed since the day before. They had added a couple of new interviews with friends and family members, but nothing groundbreaking.

I was reading through one of them when my phone rang. The text on the display simply said UNKNOWN, and I picked it up. As I suspected, it was Al since she always hid her number somehow and made sure she was untraceable. Al was what I would define as slightly paranoid and always believed someone was listening in on her conversations or looking for her.

"Stop by today," she said. "I have news for you."

Then she hung up. Thinking now would be as good a time as any, I started up the minivan and drove out across the bridges to the beachside. I wasn't planning on staying long since I wasn't going to make the same mistake I did the day before and not be there when school was out. William had tennis lessons today, I believed. Or was it violin? I couldn't really care enough to remember.

"Hi there, stranger," I said as Al cracked the door open, staring at me suspiciously before letting me in like she wanted to make sure it was really me and not some robot the government had sent to get to her.

Once inside, I closed the door behind me and walked up to her desk with her five computer screens. Some of them were showing surveillance cameras from some street somewhere in the world where it was way colder than here, judging from what people walking past the camera there wore. In one of them, they drove on the other side of the road. There was even a camera from inside a workplace somewhere, and that had me puzzled. Part of me wanted to ask why she was looking at that but decided against it. She wouldn't tell me anyway.

"So, what have you got?" I asked hopefully.

"I went through all of her stuff," Al said, "and I found that she had been Snapchatting with someone right before she disappeared. Now, your tech department wouldn't know how to regenerate old Snapchat, or they might be too lazy to, but I did. And here's a series of snaps that were sent the day before she disappeared that I think you might find interesting. I made an entire transcript in print as I know you're old-fashioned like that."

She handed me a folder.

"Thank you," I said, feeling slightly old.

"Anytime," she said. "Just let me know."

"You're the best."

I hugged her and held her tight for a few seconds, remembering the day I had caught the guy who killed her sister. After that, I never had to ask twice for her help on anything. I had earned myself a lifetime of favors, she said.

I intended to hold her to that promise.

## Chapter 24

SHE HAD SEEN him in the hallway between classes, then run into the bathroom to hide, hoping to dodge him. Heart pounding, she hurried into the girls' bathroom and into a stall, locking the door. Her legs beneath her were shaking, her breath ragged.

She sat on the toilet for a few minutes, then she heard the door leading to the hallway open and shut again. From underneath the door to her stall, she saw a set of white sneakers walk past her and then enter the one next to her, closing the door.

Sophia was still crying, so she wasn't ready to go back yet, but knew she'd have to soon. She just couldn't stand sitting there in Spanish class, where William also was, his eyes staring at her constantly whenever the teacher wasn't looking. She felt his glare on her skin, and it made the hairs stand up on her neck. He terrified her so much; she couldn't focus. It was like it would never stop. Not even after she promised him she'd keep her mouth shut. It was like he enjoyed torturing her...like he wouldn't stop because he was having so much fun. She wasn't sure she'd be able to take much more from him. It was only in this darn bathroom that he couldn't get to her.

In here, she was safe.

But it wouldn't last. At one point soon, she'd have to leave again and face him. They had Spanish together next. Sophia sighed deeply, then looked at her watch. She was going to have to be late for class, even if it got her in trouble. She couldn't risk him talking to her again. He'd only hurt her or threaten her, telling her she was worthless and that no one would listen to what she had to say. Some days, he would tell her how fat and ugly she was, or point out a pimple she had, telling her how disgusting that was. Stuff like that to make sure her confidence dropped so that she would feel worthless.

*You can't let it go on like this. You have to do something.*

Sophia shook her head. It was no use. There was no stopping William Covington. All she could do was survive, get by the best she could.

Hearing the bell ring, Sophia left the stall, then approached the sink where she splashed water on her face, hoping that it would wash away any trace of her crying. There was nothing worse than when people could tell that you had been crying. It was the worst. You couldn't break down; you had to keep up that happy face, pretending like everything was okay.

It was the unwritten rule of high school. They all did it, no matter how bad they were hurting, you knew never to show it. Whatever you did, this was the most important part.

Sophia breathed in deeply, splashing water on her face, then wiped it with paper towels and looked at her face in the mirror.

She stared at it with small gasping sounds. What she

saw in there, who she saw standing behind her in that mirror, made her heart drop instantly.

She shook her head desperately while tears sprang to her eyes, tears she knew no water could ever wash away again.

"No, please," she said. "Please, don't."

An arm reached out and grabbed her around the neck, and a knife was placed on the skin of her throat. The person stared into her eyes as the blade was pressed against her skin. As the swift movement was made, and her throat slit, blood spurted out on the mirror in front of her. Sophia gurgled, her body jolting in spasms before it fell to the ground, rag-doll limp.

The white sneakers walked away, leaving the bathroom and hurried into the crowd outside rushing to class. No one even noticed how the sneakers were now stained with blood.

## Chapter 25

I STILL HAD plenty of time, so I drove through South Beach, then found a small park where I stopped the mini-van. I grabbed the folder that Al had made, then read through the chats that she had regenerated.

I had to admit; what I read was quite a surprise, and I had to reread it a few times over to make sure I wasn't mistaken. But it did provide me with something very important that I hadn't known before.

I knew where Lucy was.

Realizing this, I put the transcripts back in the folder, then started the minivan back up. I looked at the clock. I had still a few hours before school was out. I was doing fine —no chance of me repeating the same mistake from the day before. I drove back across the bridges, then stopped at a red light when I received a text from Josie.

I JUST SPILLED CHOCOLATE MILK ALL OVER MY SHIRT. PLEASE HELP.

I exhaled and looked at the text once more. I could have told her she'd be fine and not to worry about it, but I knew how much something like this could destroy someone in eighth grade, then wrote back:

I'LL BRING YOU A NEW ONE.

I turned the minivan left instead of right, then drove back to my own house and rushed inside. I ran up the stairs and into Josie's room, opened the closet doors, then stopped. I stared at all the clothes in there, realizing I had no idea what to pick. What did Josie like out of all these shirts? There were so many to choose from?

"Need help?"

I turned to see Jean. She was holding a basket of laundry under her arm. "I was just finishing up a load and putting this back."

"Josie spilled chocolate milk on her shirt and wants me to bring her a new one."

Jean's face lit up. "Look who is trying to be father of the year."

"I just want to help her," I said.

Jean smiled. The sight of it made my heart melt. I loved her smile. It made me feel at home.

"Of course, you did. But now you have no idea what a fourteen-year-old girl would want to wear, do you?"

I grimaced. "Could you help?"

Jean chuckled, then put the basket down and walked to the closet. She pulled out a hoodie with some print on it.

"She wears this one a lot. It's her favorite anime character from *My Hero Academia*."

I stared at the hoodie. "I swear I have never seen her wear this."

Jean gave me a look. "Really? Have you ever looked at your daughter?"

I exhaled deeply. "I guess not enough. Does that mean I'm doing a horrible job of being a father? I mean, I should notice these things, shouldn't I? It's important to a young girl?"

"Eh, you're not doing too bad, Detective. The girl adores you. You're fine."

I grabbed the shirt from Jean's hand, then leaned over and kissed her forehead. "Thank you. You're a lifesaver, again."

She blushed and pulled back.

"I am sorry," I said. "Did I do something wrong?"

Jean stared at me; her lips pulled slightly apart. Then she stood on her tippy toes, closed her eyes, and leaned in for a kiss.

## Chapter 26

VALERIE HAMPTON WAS BORED. She grabbed her phone and looked at it under the table in the middle of class. She texted Ronald, and, as he had answered, Valerie raised her hand.

"Yes?" the teacher, Mr. James, said.

"Can I get a hall pass? I need to go to the bathroom."

Her teacher sighed. "That's the third time this week, Valerie."

"I know, but I really have to go; I am sorry." She held a hand to her stomach to pretend to be sick, and he finally gave in.

"All right, but maybe you should have a doctor take a look at this. It shouldn't keep being an issue."

Valerie stood to her feet. "It's okay, Mr. James. It's just that time of the month, you know."

That made the class burst into laughter, and Mr. James blush. He looked away, flustered. "All right but hurry up. I don't want you to miss out on the next part I'm getting to."

"Of course not, Mr. James," she said, batting her eyelashes. "I'll be right back."

Valerie walked into the hallway, a grin on her face. She spotted Ronald as he came around the corner, signaling for her to follow him. They couldn't risk running into any of the teachers or the SRO officer on their way, so they rushed ahead till they reached the lockers, where they stopped behind one. No one could usually see them when hiding there.

"Gosh, I thought Mr. James was never going to let me out," she whispered.

Ronald placed a finger on her lips to shut her up, then pressed her up against the wall behind her and placed his lips on top of hers and forced his tongue into her mouth. Valerie laughed and kissed him back, rolling her tongue around his like he had taught her. Ronald wasn't the first boy Valerie had kissed in the hallways of school, but he was by far the most experienced. He was a senior where she was a sophomore, and he knew a little more about life than she did. And about kissing. He knew a lot about that.

"God, you taste like cherries," he whispered, then bit her earlobe.

Valerie wasn't sure why he did that, but it made her giggle.

"What's going on back there? Who's there?"

The voice was Officer Martin's, their SRO officer. He had to have heard them.

"Shoot," Ronald said with a chuckle. "What do we do?"

Valerie looked to her right. The girl's bathroom was only a few feet away. If she could make it in there, he couldn't follow or accuse her of anything.

She giggled, then kissed Ronald's lips again before she took off, running down the hallway as fast as her legs were capable of, while she could hear Officer Martin yelling behind her.

"Hey, you two, where are you going?"

Valerie wasn't sure where Ronald had gone but assumed he had figured out for himself how to get to safety and not to be found. Or else he could talk his way out of trouble. Ronald was smart like that.

Hoping that Officer Martin hadn't seen her, she rushed into the bathroom, panting, and closed the door behind her. Then she laughed and slid to the floor when she realized she had sat in something liquid. She reached and down to feel it, then lifted her hand and looked at it. That was when her eyes fell on something—or someone—lying on the floor by the sinks.

"What the…?"

## Chapter 27

THE KISS WAS WONDERFUL; no, it was more than that...it was unearthly. Soft and gentle, and Jean tasted every bit as wonderful as I had ever dreamt she would. Everything about this moment was so incredible; I wanted it to last forever.

But it was wrong. It was wrong on so many levels, and we both knew it. I grabbed her by the shoulders and pulled her away. She opened her eyes with a small gasp and looked at me, startled.

"Jean...I..."

She shook her head, clasping her mouth, then pulled away from me. "No...No...I don't know why I did that. I am so...I should go. Your dad will be here soon and take care of Camille till you're done working. I should...probably..."

"Jean...please..."

But she had already turned around on her heel and was rushing out the door. She left me in my daughter's room, holding a black hoodie with some Japanese cartoon character that I didn't even recognize, feeling baffled. I stumbled backward and sat on the bed, then touched my lips gently. I couldn't stop thinking about that kiss and how wonderful it had felt.

But it also filled me with such a profound amount of guilt, it almost hurt.

I grabbed the hoodie and hurried into our bedroom, where Camille was. I sighed with sadness when I saw her in there. The sunlight fell on her face and made her eyes gleam, so I could see that beauty in them that I had loved so much.

I grabbed her hand in mine and kissed it. "I am so sorry, Camille; I didn't mean for it to happen. I am so, so sorry. You have no idea how terrible I feel."

Camille stared into the nothingness, as usual. I touched her cheek while my eyes filled with tears.

"I just wished I knew if it was worth it, you know? If I knew you'd ever come back to me. Is it even a life worth living? Is the life you have right now even worth living? I wish you could tell me, Camille. Because I want to know. Is it a good life? Are you happy? What will happen to you when you grow old? Do you want to if it means just continuing like this?"

I sat there, crying for a few minutes, not knowing what to do. A text from Josie pulled me out of my self-pity.

ARE YOU COMING?

I chuckled and wiped away my tears. Never a dull moment when you had kids. Especially not when you were alone with them.

I leaned over and kissed my wife, then realized a couple of tears had escaped her eyes and were rolling down her cheeks. It happened from time to time, and the doctor said it was PBA, pseudobulbar affect, a neurological condition often seen in patients with traumatic brain injury. It wasn't a sign of emotions or of her being able to see or hear us.

But it still got to me every time.

I reached over for a tissue and wiped them away, then kissed her again before rushing out the door, my phone vibrating in my pocket with the many texts from my impatient daughter, or at least I thought that's what it was.

# Chapter 28

I KNEW something was wrong from the moment I turned onto the street leading up to the high school. I had been at my daughter's school and given the shirt to the lady at the front office so Josie could grab it between classes. I had thought I was making good time, that I was doing well when I saw the blinking lights.

*What is going on?*

They had set up a perimeter all around the school, and I had to park down the road and walk the rest of the way up. A crowd had gathered, women mostly, and I guessed they were mothers who lived close by, and who heard the rumors first.

I found my way through and went up to the officer guarding the entrance. He saw me and recognized me, then let me through.

A sensation of anxiety rumbled in my stomach as I walked in through the doors, nodding politely at the colleagues I met on the way. I grabbed my phone and looked at the display, then realized Fowler had called five times.

*This can't be good.*

I barely made it inside the hallway before I heard his voice, growling my name. I turned my head and saw him come running toward me.

"Hunter!"

Fowler was a big guy like me, not quite as tall, so I could still look down on him when he spoke, but he was pretty sizable in stature and pretty intimidating, especially with his scowling look. The very same look he was giving me right now.

"Where have you been?"

I opened my mouth to answer, but he had no time to wait for me to find the words before he continued.

"Weren't you supposed to be here? Because I vividly remember telling you to stay with William Covington all day, didn't I?"

I nodded. "Yes, sir. I had an emergency at home."

He huffed. "What else is new, right?"

"I have a sick wife; you know this, Fowler."

He paused, then rubbed his forehead. "I know. I know. I am sorry. It's just…well, I can't trust you anymore. You're always running around, and I never know where you are these days. How could this happen on your watch?"

I took in a deep breath. I hated to use Camille as an excuse, but right now, I had to. I couldn't afford to lose my job. Fowler was trying hard not to let his frustration run away with him. I could tell by the way he clenched his fists.

"Well, I'm here now. What happened?" I asked.

Fowler exhaled. "Come with me."

I followed him down the hallway and to the girls' bathroom. The door was open, and I looked inside just in time to see a young girl being pulled onto a stretcher and rushed out of there by paramedics.

"That's a lot of blood," I said, feeling sick. This was awful.

"He cut her throat," Fowler said.

"Knife?"

"We found this," Fowler said and lifted an evidence bag with a bloody fishing knife inside of it.

I walked closer to the area, then knelt next to the pool of blood. "Same type of knife as on the boat, huh? I almost don't dare to ask…"

Fowler nodded. He pulled out another bag and showed it to me. It contained a small black chess piece, a knight.

"We found it in her hand. He must have placed it there before he took off."

I stared at the chess piece, then wondered if William Covington was a chess player. I would bet my right arm he was.

Fowler escorted me out and down the hallway, then stopped. "Listen, Hunter. You know I love you, man; we've known each other for what feels like forever. But I can't keep covering for you. This happened on your watch, and you weren't here. You've got to step up. Now, it wasn't William Covington who was hurt…this time, so I'll let this one slide, but this is your last chance. Do you hear me? Any more slip-ups and you're out. William's dad is a very important contributor to Mayor Simon's campaign. He's a big deal around here, and if anything happens to his son, we'll all lose our jobs; do you understand?"

"Listen, Fowler; I might have found some important information in the case…"

Fowler raised his finger. He puffed himself up while looking at me, a vein popping out in his forehead.

"There is no case for you; do you hear me? Morales and his team are on it. You focus on keeping the boy safe. That is all. Understood?"

I nodded. "Understood."

"Good," Fowler said and left me. As I watched him walk down the hallway, I spotted someone rushing by me and recognized his face immediately.

"Mr. James?"

I hurried up next to him. He seemed in a rush to get away, but I stopped him. "Please, I need to talk to you. Here's my card. Call me, and we'll talk."

He stopped, then looked around to see if anyone saw us together, taking the card from my hand.

"You're a teacher here, aren't you?" I asked.

He nodded. "Yes. What is it you want?"

"That thing yesterday. What was it about?"

His eyes avoided mine. "Please, Detective, I don't want any trouble. Just leave me alone; will you?"

He began to walk toward the exit, and I followed him out into the parking lot. "I told the police everything I knew. They said I could go," he said. "I don't know why you keep following me."

"I want to talk about last night. Why was William Covington at your home? What did he want, and why was he hurting you?"

James shook his head and crossed the parking lot. "I don't know what you're talking about. I was with my family last night. We had dinner; we watched SpongeBob."

"Come on, Mr. James. I was there. I saw him. I saw what happened, what he did to you. Why don't you report him?"

James stopped in his tracks. He turned around to confront me, his face strained with anger, cheeks blushing, and eyes ablaze.

"You listen to me, Detective. You leave this alone, or I'll report you for misconduct. All I want is for you to leave me alone; do you think you can do that?"

And with that, he turned back around and walked up to his car and got in. He roared it to life, then drove past me, giving me an angry glare through the window. As the car disappeared, I turned around to go back when I spotted William standing by the wall of the school, leaning against it, his eyes lingering on me, a sly smile on his lips. The rage in his eyes made my blood run cold.

## Chapter 29

JEAN DROVE TOWARD THE HOSPITAL, thinking about Harry. It wasn't that unusual for her to do that since he was constantly on her mind. She was always thinking about him, but today, a little more than usual. Today, she didn't want to think about him; she wanted to forget he even existed. She was so angry at herself for kissing him like that. It was something she had promised herself never to let happen, yet she had done it anyway. Out of the blue? It made no sense.

*Have you no self-control?*

Jean felt so ashamed of herself that she, for a moment, considered running away, moving away from town, or at least from the neighborhood, so she wouldn't have to face him again. Could she ever look into his eyes again?

She wasn't sure.

But the kiss had been wonderful. She had to admit it had been better than she had ever imagined it would be, and she had thought about kissing him a lot. She had tried hard not to for years, trying to push the thought away, but it had been on her mind a lot anyway, what it would be like to kiss Harry.

Why couldn't he have been an awful kisser? Why did he have to have such wonderfully soft lips?

Jean wasn't happy to admit it but kissing Harry had been on her mind even before Camille overdosed. That was the worst part of it all. Jean had always liked Harry, and she had always felt there was a connection between them, one she had never had with anyone else in the world. But he had belonged to Camille, and he still did, even if she was foolish enough to take those drugs. Thinking about it made Jean so angry.

Didn't she know she had it all?

"What could you possibly have been sad about? What could you possibly have wanted to escape from, huh?" she said into the car as if Camille were still there. "You weren't lonely like me. You weren't scared of never finding anyone who would love you. You had someone who adored your every step. You had everything...the most wonderful man in the world, the sweetest kid. Why would you do this to yourself? You had everything, literally everything I ever wanted."

Jean slammed her hand into the steering wheel as she drove into the parking lot of South Miami Hospital and stopped the car. She grabbed her purse, then looked in the mirror, correcting her hair and makeup.

"You're such a fool, Jean. You've ruined everything," she told herself with a deep sigh, then left the car and rushed inside.

She had just started her shift when they needed her right away. Jean had barely put her bag down when she had to rush into the ER. A young girl was coming in, someone said.

Jean ran down the hallway and was ready as they rolled her inside.

"Girl, eighteen, someone slit her throat with a knife," the paramedics said as they ran down the hallway. "Luckily, a girl found her right after it happened and tried to stop the bleeding with her shirt. She's lost a lot of blood. I'm not sure she's gonna make it."

# Chapter 30

I KNEW I was jeopardizing everything, but I had to follow my instincts, and that was to find Lucy Lockwood as soon as possible. So, I took off, not caring what happened to William Covington, or what he was up to. I knew I had just promised my boss something else, but I'd have to deal with that later.

Instead, I drove downtown, growling in anger, Al's folder lying on the passenger seat beside me. Here, another girl had been attacked, and my boss wouldn't even listen to what I had to say.

I drove over the bridge and north onto the beach, then stopped in front of a condominium where I parked the car. I looked at the building in front of me, then at the folder, and the transcripts from her Snapchat.

I walked out and up to the front entrance, then spotted someone coming out and went to hide around the corner.

The woman didn't see me. She walked past me on her high heels, tapping along on the asphalt, seemingly in a rush.

I turned the corner and approached her.

"Mrs. Lockwood?"

She turned to look at me with a gasp. Then she forced a smile.

"Detective Hunter. W-what are you doing here?"

I smiled back, mirroring her fake smile. "Well, I was in the neighborhood, and I thought I'd stop by and say hello to Lucy."

"L-Lucy?"

Valentina Lockwood was many things, but an actress wasn't one of them.

"Let's cut the crap, shall we?" I said. "I know that she's up there in your apartment that is in your maiden name, Valentina Gómez. I read about it all in those Snapchats you thought had been deleted…the ones between you and Lucy planning this. Your husband doesn't know about it; does he? When did you buy it?"

She stared at me, the mask coming off. Her nostrils were flaring angrily, yet I could tell she knew she was defeated.

"He doesn't know, no. I bought it when I decided to leave him two years ago after he…"

I reached over and pulled the edge of her shirt to the side, revealing a huge purple bruise on her chest.

"How long has this been going on?"

She pulled back. "For as long as I can remember. He's always been like this, but it's getting worse. I thought I could leave him, but I don't know how…I bought the condo with my own money that my mother sent me and kept it just in case I finally managed to gain the courage."

"And she's up there? She's been there the entire time?" I asked. "Let me guess; Mr. Lockwood isn't very happy about what happened to her, and he blames her?"

Mrs. Lockwood looked down, then nodded like she was the one who was the bad guy. I had seen so many women like her in my line of work. They were trapped. There was nowhere for them to go, completely dependent on their husbands who treated them like dirt. I couldn't stand it.

"And the baby? William's child?"

Valentina bit her lip. "Robert wanted to kill it. He wanted her to get an abortion. I couldn't let him."

"So, you faked her disappearance?" I asked.

She nodded. "Yes. Please, don't tell him. Please, I beg of you."

I ran a hand through my hair. "I won't. But I'll probably need to talk to her."

## Chapter 31

SHE SURVIVED THE SURGERY. How that was even possible with the condition she was in when she got to the hospital was beyond Jean, but she had. Sophia Fisher was in the ICU now on life-support and in critical condition, but alive.

*We saved one of your girls, Harry.*

It wasn't hard for Jean to figure out that this girl had to do with Harry's case. She didn't know the details of it, but Harry had told her about the girls who were killed on the boat and the one that was found in the dumpster. This incident had happened at the same school that all the others went to and where Harry spent his day protecting the kid that they believed had raped the girl that disappeared.

"We're gonna get you up and running in no time," Jean said as she checked Sophia's vitals.

Jean worked the ICU from time to time, and since there was a lack of nurses in the ICU today with the many patients that had come in, she had volunteered to help. They had assigned her to Sophia.

Now, she stared at the girl who lay in the bed, her eyes closed, fighting for her life. It was an awful sight, yet Jean found it to be hopeful. The girl had made it this far, and she would do her very best to make sure she made it all the way.

"You and me, we're tough girls," she said to her, "Nothing gets us down."

*Except Harry.*

Jean sighed when thinking about him again and looked out the window. The sun was setting on the Intracoastal waters, creating a gorgeous light.

"Why can't it be us?" she mumbled as though Sophia could hear or even cared. "She had her chance, and she blew it. Now, she's gone; she just lays up there, a vegetable, and meanwhile, we walk around each other, wanting it to be more, but unable to do anything about it. It's not fair, you know? I know; I know what you'll say…life's not fair and all that. I know, I know. I shouldn't feel sorry for myself, yet sometimes I really do. I take care of that woman day and night. I change her catheter; I wash her in parts only her husband should see. I make sure she's kept alive and that she can stay in the house with him. Why? Because I love him. Because I want to do this for him, I want to help him. And maybe because I feel awful for not being able to help her, for not seeing that she was back on the drugs. But does that mean I should just stop living my own life? Don't I have a right to be loved too?"

Jean felt tears pile up in her eyes and then let the tears roll down her cheeks. She wasn't usually one to feel sorry for herself, but today, she was. Today, she felt like everything had exploded in her face and that there was no turning back. She had kissed him, and that opened up a whole can of worms. There was no taking it back. All she wanted was to be happy. Was that so terrible?

Jean wiped her eyes on her sleeve with a sniffle, then shook her head. "I'm sorry to be telling you all this. It's not really your problem anyway. And, frankly, I'm being a baby. I could just go out and find some other guy, right? I could find someone who is actually available instead of wasting all my time and energy on someone who never will be. You're right."

Jean turned to look at Sophia, then smiled when the girl suddenly moved in her bed and groaned. Jean's eyes grew wide open, and she approached her.

"Sophia?"

The girl moved her head from side to side, moaning loudly like she was having a bad dream. Was she waking up?

"Sophia?"

The girl opened her mouth and mumbled something. It was impossible for Jean to make out what it was, so she moved closer, so close she could hear her even when she whispered.

And what she heard made her heart race in her chest so violently it hurt.

## Chapter 32

THE TWO-BEDROOM APARTMENT on the seventeenth floor had gorgeous views over the glistening Atlantic Ocean. It was nicely decorated in blue and white, making it seem like a truly relaxing beach retreat. A lamp made of shells dangled calmly from the ceiling. A huge painting of a sea turtle brought the ocean inside.

On the floor of the living room was a young girl and a young child, both sitting on the carpet.

"Did you forget something?" she yelled without turning to look at us.

"Lucy?" I said and stepped forward. She turned her head and looked up at me, her eyes confused. I recognized her from the many pictures I had seen in the police reports and in the articles I had read about the rape and her disappearance.

Lucy looked at her mother, who was standing right behind me. "W-what…who is he, Mom?"

"It's okay, Lucy," Valentina said. "He knows. He's not gonna harm either of you or take the child. He just wants to talk to you. It's okay, Lucy; trust me."

Lucy eased up slightly. She still looked at me suspiciously.

I stepped forward. "My name is Detective Harry Hunter. I've been looking for you, Lucy."

Lucy scoffed and turned to look at the baby as she fussed. Lucy helped her get the small wooden toy she couldn't reach. I was suddenly taken back to when Josie had been the same age and remembered her dependence on her surroundings, especially on her mother. It was truly magical that such a small helpless creature could grow into what Josie was today. And, frankly, I hadn't done much but keep her alive.

"Precious," I said and squatted next to Lucy, nodding toward the baby. "What's her name?"

"Isabella, like my grandmother," Lucy said, smiling in that way only a mother could when looking at her child. It was obvious she was tired from lack of sleep and constantly being on watch, but she still had that peace over her that only a new mother had.

"Beautiful," I said. "She's big and sitting by herself, huh? I remember that as being a relief for my wife when our daughter started sitting up on her own. That meant you didn't have to hold her constantly anymore."

Lucy chuckled. "Yeah, that is a help. But she keeps throwing those blocks away and then wanting them back, so I have to get them for her...see? She did it again."

The block dropped to the floor, and Isabella made sounds while drool ran down her chin. Lucy wiped her daughter's mouth, then grabbed the block, and gave it to her again. This time, the girl bit into it.

"Teething, huh?" I asked. "That's probably disturbing her sleep, am I right?"

"Oh, my God, constantly," Lucy said. "She cried almost all night."

"Any of them poking through yet?"

"One of the lower front teeth has just poked through the gums; I think it hurts because she bites into everything these days."

I nodded and chuckled. "You can buy these cooling toys that you put in the freezer; when they bite into them, it helps soothe the pain. Josie used to love those."

"I'll remember that," Lucy said. "So…what can I do for you, Detective? I assume you didn't come here to talk about baby teeth?"

I smiled. "Well…no. I need to talk to you. See, there are a lot of people looking for you. Have you heard about the kids that were killed on the boat? They were all from your school. There was also someone they found in a dumpster."

Lucy nodded. Her eyes hit the floor. "I've seen a little bit about it on TV when Isabella has been asleep."

"So, you also know that all those girls that have been killed were on the list of people who witnessed what happened to you on the beach."

"You mean when I was raped," she said, changing expression, her eyes suddenly filled with deep anger.

"Yes," I said.

"I know," she said sadly.

"Okay, so, now you might understand when I tell you that we have been looking for you in connection with these murders."

She wrinkled her forehead. The baby fussed and started biting her hand instead of the block.

"No, why is that?"

"Well, the killings seem to be connected to what happened that night, and to be completely honest with you…"

She laughed. It took me by surprise. "They think I'm

killing them? Because they wouldn't testify? That's ridiculous." She grabbed her baby and held her up. "I have kind of been busy with something else here."

"But, I have to ask you where you were on Saturday night between eight p.m. and midnight when the bodies were found?"

"Where I was? Where do you think I was? Where do I spend all my days and nights? I was right here, of course, taking care of this baby that I didn't ask for because this is my life now. While all my friends are out being young and partying, I'm stuck here with her for the rest of my life. Not that I ever partied when I could, but I would at least like to be able to go out."

"Did anyone see you? Your mom, was she here? Is there a doorman who can say you didn't leave the condo?"

"I was...at home," Valentina said. "And we don't have a doorman. But Lucy only leaves the place when she takes Isabella for walks or when they go to the beach. I bring her groceries, or she orders take-out."

"Did you order take-out that night?"

"I might have. I think I ordered a pizza. It's what I eat most nights anyway before I pass out as soon as she falls asleep. No, wait, I didn't order pizza on Saturday because I had Chinese leftovers from the night before."

I rose to my feet, standing up straight. "I see. I just... well, I need to figure out how to explain it all to my superiors."

"Maybe you just don't," she said and stood up, holding Isabella on her hip. "I don't want anyone to know where I am or that I have a child. Just tell them I left the state, and I won't be back."

"I'm not sure it's that easy. They will find you at some point," I said, walking toward the door. A wooden chessboard with the black and white pieces on top of it stood on a small end table. None of the pieces were missing. "But, I guess I'll just have to come up with something."

I stopped and looked at the boardgame.

"Who plays chess?"

"Lucy was state champion," her mother said proudly.

"That was years ago," Lucy said and looked away. "In another lifetime."

## Chapter 33

JEAN TRIED TO CALL HARRY, but as usual, it went straight to voicemail. What was it with him and cell-phones? He had to be the only guy in this century that was impossible to reach. Harry never picked up his phone and always kept it on silent; it was annoying, especially now that Jean really needed to get ahold of him.

*Come on, Harry, pick up!*

When she got voicemail again, Jean growled and put the phone down. This wasn't the kind of stuff you told to voicemail. It was too important. She wondered if she should get in her car and drive down to the high school and look for him, but she still had several hours left of her shift and couldn't just leave. The patients needed her.

"Why do you have to make everything so difficult, Harry?" she mumbled as she put the phone back in the chest pocket of her scrubs. She walked down the hallway, and as she passed Sophia's room, she saw movement. The door was open, so she peeked inside, an uneasy sensation growing inside of her.

"Hello?"

A shadow moved by the wall, and Jean's heart dropped. "Who...wh...?"

A person wearing a doctor's coat was bent over Sophia's body, and at first, Jean thought something had happened to her, but then she saw the plastic bag wrapped around Sophia's face.

"Hey, what are you doing? STOP!"

Jean sprang forward, grabbed the person by the collar and pulled it forcefully. The person stumbled backward but managed to push Jean off, and she slid backward across the floor, hitting her back against something hard. Sophia's body was jerking in the bed, and Jean began to scream.

"HELP! SOMEONE HELP!"

Jean stood to her feet, then lunged forward, plunging into this person with all her weight. She grabbed the attacker around the neck with her arm and pulled with all her might. The attacker gasped as she pulled and pulled till the hands let go of the plastic bag while she still screamed for help.

"HELP. IN HERE. HELP!"

Jean stared at Sophia while fighting the attacker, who was struggling to hold onto the squirming body. Sophia wasn't moving in the bed; her chest wasn't heaving up and down like it was supposed to.

*Was I too late? Is she still breathing?*

The attacker tried to fight loose from her grip and managed to push an elbow into Jean's stomach so hard that she let go with a loud yelp. The attacker then turned around, grabbed Jean, and slammed a fist into her face, repeating it three times. Pain shot through her jaw and into her brain. She saw stars and felt her body fall to the ground, then slide across the tiles. She heard footsteps in the distance, then yelling, and sensed her attacker going into panic. She then felt hands on her body. She tried to scream for help, but nothing came out. At least she didn't think it did. As she was put into a wheelchair and rolled off down the hallway, Jean was slowly fading off into the unknown.

## Chapter 34

MY DAD WAS SITTING in the living room when I got back, watching the news on TV. I kissed his forehead and then went into the kitchen to unload the groceries. I had promised Josie I'd make my famous meatloaf for dinner, her favorite. Big Daddy's Killer Meatloaf...she had named it a couple of years ago. It was actually my mom's recipe, but I knew that she wouldn't mind if I took the credit.

We sat down to eat, the three of us, with Josie trying to look at her phone under the table, thinking I didn't see her.

"Josie," I said and nodded toward the phone in her hand. "Not at the table."

She put it down with a deep sigh, and my dad blessed the food.

"Thank you, God, for this wonderful food and the wonderful company. Thank you for blessing us all and for taking good care of Ellen till we can be with her again. Amen."

"Amen," I said and nodded at Josie to begin serving herself some food.

"Finally," she exclaimed and cut a huge chunk of the meatloaf and put it on her plate. "I'm starving."

My dad chuckled when seeing her plate getting filled and her throwing herself at it like she hadn't seen food for days. I remembered that kind of appetite at her age when I was shooting up like a rocket too. It was hard to explain to your smaller friends, but you needed loads of food when growing that fast, and being hungry felt like you would die. I often came close to passing out in those days.

"No Jean tonight?" my dad said after a few bites.

I froze when hearing her name mentioned. I had to admit; I was happy she wasn't here tonight. I wouldn't know how to face her after what had happened earlier in the day. What would I say to her? She had rushed out, completely out of it. Not that I felt like she needed to be. It wasn't her fault. We had both wanted this to happen.

"I think she's working," I said, hoping he'd change the subject.

"I'm done. Can I be excused?" Josie said and grabbed her phone. I had the feeling she had hurried up to finish eating as fast as possible, so she could get back on her phone, texting her friends, or watching videos or whatever she was doing. I gave her a concerned look, the "daddy look," as she called it.

"You sure you had enough to eat? You know how easily you get hungry an hour after dinner because you didn't eat enough."

She shrugged and got up with the phone in her hand. "I'll just grab some chips or something then."

She rushed up, running past me, but I stopped her.

"Plate," I said. "It won't find its way to the dishwasher on its own."

She groaned loudly, sounding like she was going to die.

I shared a look with my dad, and he lifted his eyebrows while Josie did as she was told. I chuckled as she left.

"And so it has begun," my dad said, drinking his sweet tea. "You ready for total and utter chaos for the next five years or so?"

I ate some of my meatloaf and mashed potatoes. "As ready as I'll ever be," I said.

"It's not gonna be easy being the only one here," he said. "Once those boys come knocking on your door...I remember when they started coming for Reese..."

He paused, then looked down. I felt a pinch in my heart. Reese wasn't doing well. I hadn't spoken to her in weeks, and neither had my dad. We were worried about her, and there wasn't a day when we both didn't wonder what her life would have turned out to be if it hadn't been for that rape.

She had never been the same afterward.

My dad leaned back in the chair and sent me a sad smile. "Anyway, I meant what I said yesterday. You really ought to do something about it before it's too late."

"About Jean?"

"Yes."

I lifted my eyebrows. "I thought we talked about this, Dad. I'm a married man. I have a wife."

He leaned forward and put his hand on my arm. "When will you realize she's not coming back? You have to let her go, son. She's gone. You heard the doctors. She's never coming back. It never happens with people in her condition. Can't you see? You're wasting away, trying to care for her, scrambling to make it all work. Yes, Jean is here to help, but for how long? Once she realizes you don't want her, she's gonna go away. And then what?

Meanwhile, you're missing out on everything. You're thirty-six for crying out loud. You're still young. You need

114

to live your life. I see the way you two look at one another, the way you talk. That kind of love is so rare. When you have it, you should hold onto it for dear life."

I exhaled tiredly. My dad had never been fond of Camille. I don't know if it was her past with the drugs or the fact that she was Caribbean. But he never really connected with her, and my mother didn't either. Still, they had always tried their best. It broke my mother's heart when she overdosed, and she helped out for a long time until she died suddenly of an aneurism while vacuuming her house. I sometimes wondered if seeing me in so much distress after Camille's overdose played a part in the aneurysm bursting.

"Don't waste any more of your life, son," he continued. "You'll only end up regretting it. You don't want that kind of regret in your life."

"So, what, you want me just to forget I have a wife upstairs? I can't do that, Dad."

"Send her to a nursing home, son. They can take care of her there. There'll be someone with her all the time, trained nurses who will be able to give her the care she needs. The way it is now, you're barely keeping it together. You're exhausted. It's too much."

I leaned back in my chair with a surprised scoff. I shook my head. "What on Earth happened to believing in miracles, Dad?"

He put his fist on the table. "She's not gonna wake up, son. You're living in a fantasy if you believe she will."

"Wow," I said as I got up and began clearing the table. I stopped with the plates in my hands, then looked down at my dad. "Well, you can think what you want, Dad. I still believe God will bring her back to me. I have faith that he will wake her up, and I want her to be here in the house, surrounded by her loved ones when it happens."

## Chapter 35

WAKING UP WAS PAINFUL. Her head was pounding. The sounds coming from outside her body felt so loud...her head was about to explode. Her entire body was hurting so badly she wanted to scream.

Yet, she couldn't.

Jean tried again, then shot her eyes wide open.

*Oh, dear God, no.*

She couldn't scream for the simple reason that she had been gagged. A wet cloth that tasted like dirty laundry had been shoved into her mouth and halfway down her throat, making her want to gag.

*Help? Someone? Anyone?*

She was lying down. Her hands had been tied, and her legs bound together. The place she was in was so tight that she could barely move.

*Where am I?*

Darkness surrounded her, and she tried to sit up but couldn't. There was no more space above her head, and she knocked into the roof.

*What is this place?*

While groaning behind the gag, she tried to move around, to turn herself so she might be able to see something, anything, but there was nothing but darkness in the tight space. In the distance somewhere, she thought she heard noises; was someone speaking? No, it was different. It was singing. It was a radio. Somewhere close by, a radio was running.

*Hello?*

She tried to get a sound out behind her gag, but it was impossible. No matter how much power she put behind it, there was nothing but muffled sounds. The wet cloth in her mouth felt like it would suffocate her. Panic set in at the thought, and her heart began hammering in her chest, knocking against her ribcage. She tried to calm herself, but it was nearly impossible. The feeling that she couldn't move caused her to lose control of herself and she hyperventilated.

She closed her eyes and cried, trying to remember what had happened…what had gone down before this moment. She remembered being in Sophia's room. She recalled there being someone in there, and then the fight. She remembered falling, and then the fist that kept coming again and again.

Was there a wheelchair? Yes, she remembered being put in one, then being rolled away. She even remembered the people she passed, trying to speak to them, to reach out or scream for help, but no sound came out of her. She remembered their eyes focused on something else, some even running, none of them noticing her. And then she remembered drifting in and out of consciousness…that alluring darkness that kept calling to her. She remembered it all like small pieces of film that she now ran for her inner eye, piecing it all together until she finally opened her eyes with a gasp for air.

Just as she did this, she heard an engine turn over and then felt the room she was in begin to move.

## Chapter 36

"I'M TELLING YOU, Camille, she's turning into a regular teenager. It's gotta be the hormones. That's the only way I can explain it. Last night, I couldn't get her to go to bed. She kept crying. Finally, I managed to calm her down and get her to talk. Apparently, she's struggling with friends at school. Her best friend, DD, has turned her back on her and is now best friends with some other girl and won't even talk to Josie at school. Now, she thinks no one likes her, that everyone thinks she's weird. It breaks my heart to see her like this. What happened to my girl who could be beaten by nothing in life? She used to be so strong. She never used to care what other people thought about her. I thought our struggle would be her stubbornness. Not this. This is nothing like what I imagined. You should have seen her, Camille. She was inconsolable, and I couldn't help her. I never thought it was going to be like this. I have no idea how to deal with stuff like that, all the drama. I'm a boy. We never had drama like that. At least none that I know of."

I sighed and looked at my wife in the darkness. She was

sleeping. At least, I thought she was. It was hard to tell. I grabbed her hand in mine and kissed the back of it.

"Gosh, I wish you were here to help me," I said and wiped away a tear. "You'd know what to do, how to help her. It doesn't matter what I say; it doesn't help anything. It usually only makes her even angrier or sadder."

I leaned back in my chair and looked out the window at the horizon. The sun had begun to rise, and it was getting lighter out. I had only slept a few hours, but I knew I wasn't going to get any more. Instead, I leaned over, kissed my wife on the forehead, then headed into the shower.

When Josie came down, I had made pancakes and bacon, thinking her favorite breakfast might cheer her up. To my surprise, she was in an excellent mood this morning and didn't mention a single word about her friends or what she had been so sad about the night before. She smiled and kissed my cheek as I served her the food. I looked at the clock and realized I had to get going if I was going to make it to the Covington house before William left for school. I was getting pretty sick of playing babysitter, but what could I do? I needed my job.

"Is Jean not coming over this morning?" Josie asked.

"I don't know, sweetie. I haven't heard from her since yesterday. She had called a few times, and when I tried to call her back last night, she didn't pick up. She might be busy," I said, then added: "Eat your breakfast. I'll stay till the bus comes if she doesn't show up."

"Who's gonna look after Mom?" she asked, concerned. "If Jean can't come today? She usually takes care of her till she needs to go to work."

I sighed, not knowing what to say. My dad could come over, but I'd have to change her feeding tube and catheter and turn her in the bed to prevent pressure sores. After that was done, my dad could easily take over.

But that meant I'd be late for work. It wasn't going to make me popular.

"I hope she's all right," Josie said and finished her orange juice. "She usually always comes over in the morning, even when she's worked night shift."

I nodded and took a bite of my pancake as well. "I know. It isn't like her. I don't know what's going on. I'm sure she's all right, though."

*But you do know, don't you? She kissed you, and the way you reacted scared her off. What if she never comes back?*

Barely had I sent Josie off with the bus when I received a text from a number I didn't know. It said:

I AM READY TO TALK. JAMES.

## Chapter 37

I SKIPPED Covington's house completely and drove directly to Howard James's address. It was close to the school, and that's where William was going to be in a few minutes anyway. I drove onto the driveway and parked, then rushed up to the house. I knocked, but no one answered. I grabbed the door handle and opened the door, then walked inside.

"Howard James? It's Harry Hunter. I came as soon as I got your text…"

I walked into the living room and found someone sitting in the kitchen.

"Howard James?"

The guy didn't look up at me. He stared at the tabletop in front of him, his head bent, his shoulders slumped. I walked up to him and sat down in a chair across from him. He finally lifted his glance and looked at me.

"They can never know."

"Who? Your family?"

He nodded. "Julia and the kids can never know."

I shook my head as my eyes fell on a picture of him and his family on the wall. The kids could be no more than three and five years old—two beautiful girls with light curly hair and broad smiles.

James grabbed my arm with his left hand and clenched it, a desperate look in his eyes. His right hand, he kept under the table.

"You must promise me they'll never know."

I looked into his eyes, then nodded. "Of course."

James eased up slightly and let go of my arm. Tears sprang to his strained red-rimmed eyes. He looked like a man who hadn't slept in weeks. He looked like a broken man about to fall apart.

"Just tell me," I said. "You need to get it off your chest."

He stared at me like he was still undecided whether he could trust me or not, then wiped his nose with his hand, sniffling.

"You're not gonna like it," he said.

"I'm sure I won't, but right now, keeping this a secret is making you sick. You can trust me."

He gave me another suspicious look, then made his decision. He leaned back with a deep sigh.

"I don't know exactly when it started. Or who came on to whom. But it happened. The very thing that can't happen when you're a teacher."

"You fell in love with a student?"

He exhaled, then nodded. "Yes. But I never wanted it to happen. You must trust me when I say that I never meant for it to go this far. It just…"

I closed my eyes briefly, thinking about my Josie. I didn't know what I'd do if I found out a teacher had…I couldn't even finish the thought.

"How far did it go?" I asked, even though I desperately didn't want to know the answer.

He gave me a look. "Too far. It went way too far. We started meeting up in secret and…"

"You slept together; I take it?" I asked.

He swallowed, then looked away.

"Okay," I said. "And I take it that William Covington found out somehow and used it against you?"

"Yes, but it's more than that. I didn't find this out until later, but he arranged the entire thing. He set me up."

I wrinkled my forehead. "How so?"

James breathed raggedly. He was a desperate man at this point.

"He…he…forced her to…to pretend like she wanted to be with me."

"Excuse me?"

"He saw how I looked at her in class, and he told her to play along. She told me this later on when we were alone, and she broke down and cried. He pressured her to sleep with me. He knew a secret of hers that would be so devastating to her and her family that it would have destroyed her life. She never told me what it was, but it was enough for her to do as he said. He trapped me, so I'd do as he told me to."

James spoke through gritted teeth, and I sensed his anger from where I was sitting.

"I'm not justifying what I did," he continued. "I knew what I did was wrong. But to find out that it was all…based on a lie? That got me so mad."

"Only now, you can't do anything about it because William Covington knows."

"He has pictures. He hid in the room. We were in her parents' house when they were out of town, and he was there too when we…and he took pictures with his phone that he has kept."

"And now he's blackmailing you? What does he want you to do?"

"Let him pass my class," James said. "It's as simple as that. He was failing, and he went this far just to pass. He's that despicable. Just for a passing grade."

"But I'm guessing he's not stopping there," I said.

"No. That was just the beginning. Now, he just enjoys torturing me for the fun of it. He shows up here and acts like he owns me. He gets me to fail people he doesn't like, or to get him stuff that he needs like alcohol, sometimes weed, stuff like that. I've become his darn puppet. That's all I am. And it won't end."

"And you can't tell the police because they'll arrest you for having sex with a minor," I said. "Why now? You know I'll have to report you after this."

Tears rolled down his face while his hand moved under the table. His eyes looked at me, pleading.

"Stop him, please. I made a mistake, and now I'm paying the price," he said, sobbing. "My family will be destroyed, and so will I. But he can't hurt anyone else. Please, stop him, please."

Seeing the deep desperation in this man's eyes almost made me lose it. "I…I can't…I mean…"

James shook his head, tears running across his cheeks. "You can't stop him, can you?"

I felt paralyzed. I had no idea what to say to him. Should I just tell him the truth, that a guy like William Covington was hard to stop, especially when no one would stand up to him and tell the truth? When he ran a regime of terror that was built on destroying everyone around him?

"If you come forward," I said. "If you tell the truth, then maybe others will…"

I said the words, but he knew I didn't believe them. I had barely finished the sentence before he shook his head, crying hard, then pulled out his hand from underneath the table. It was too late when I realized it was holding a gun.

## Chapter 38

JAMES PLACED the gun on his temple and pulled the trigger. It all went by so fast; I hardly even managed to react. The bullet blasted half of his face to pieces, and he fell to the table with a thud, slamming what was left of him into the wood.

I was paralyzed with shock.

I was barely breathing.

Just like that, a life was over. Just like that, two children were fatherless, and a wife had become a widow.

It was unbearable to even think about.

I stared at the body in front of me, then down at the blood that had sprayed my shirt and my hands. I was shaking, trembling, half crying, half choking. I was hyperventilating, my eyes staring at Howard James lying there, lifeless.

*Oh, dear God, no.*

When I finally was able to gather myself, I grabbed my phone out of my pocket and called for first responders, frantically tapping the display, speaking through tears as the call finally went through.

It took less than twenty minutes before Fowler was standing in the doorway, looking at me. I had been talking to the paramedics until then, and now my colleagues entered.

"What the heck do you think you're doing?" Fowler asked, raging. "Where's the boy? Where's William Covington?"

"He's at school up the street. I was here to talk to…one of the teachers. He had something he needed to talk to me about. It was important."

"Important enough for you to leave your post?"

I nodded. "Yes."

Fowler growled. "Need I remind you that you're not working a case here?"

"No…but…"

"You're in the business of protecting. Why are you interviewing teachers?"

I stared at him, then shook my head. "You know what? I just watched a guy, a father, take his own life. I am not going to stand here being talked to like I'm a baby," I said. "Fire me if you have to."

I pushed myself past him, out the door, while he turned to look after me.

"You bet I will. You're out, Hunter!"

I paused, took in a deep breath, and closed my eyes for a brief second. I wondered if there was anything I needed to say…if I should ask for his forgiveness for the sake of my family's survival, but then decided against it. I was done with this game. I didn't owe him anything. Instead, I continued on my way outside. The sky had grown dark, and black clouds had gathered above me like they knew how I felt.

I was angry. No, it was more than that. I was good old fashioned pissed off. I was sick of this boy and what I had learned about him. I was done with protecting him. And I was going to make sure he was done terrorizing people. Fowler had fired me. I had nothing more to lose.

If I was going down, then I was taking him down with me.

## Chapter 39

I DROVE AWAY from the scene after giving my testimony to one of my colleagues, telling him the details of what had happened. Then I rushed back to my car and took off. Luckily, I had a jacket in the car that I put on to hide the blood on my white shirt. I didn't want to scare people. I then walked into the school and into the front office. I showed the lady sitting there my badge. She stared at it, startled.

"I need to see William Covington. Now, please."

The lady behind the desk nodded nervously, then grabbed the phone and called a number.

"Yes, could I have William Covington come to the front office, please? There's someone here to see him."

I stared at her round face and narrow-set eyes as she listened, then nodded. "Okay, I see."

She hung up and looked at me. "William left early. No one has seen him since third period."

I lifted my eyebrows, surprised. "He left early?"

"That's what they said. He didn't sign out with me,

though, as he is supposed to. He's not allowed just to leave."

"So, you don't know where he is?" I asked.

She shook her head. "I'm afraid not."

"And he couldn't be in some other class?"

"He's supposed to be in Math, and he wasn't. When the teacher asked about him, someone said William left after third period. That's all I know."

I exhaled, confused. "Okay. Thank you."

"I'm sorry I couldn't be of more help."

"That's okay," I said, my pulse quickening. Something wasn't right here. I could sense it; something was awfully wrong.

I thanked her again, then left, rushing outside. I was on my way to the minivan when I thought of something. Call it instinct or maybe just a hunch, but something seemed to be very off here. There was one thing I needed to check before I left. I hurried across the parking lot, where I found William's Range Rover still in its usual spot.

"That's odd," I mumbled, then walked up to it, thinking maybe he was still sitting inside and hadn't taken off yet. Or perhaps he had just come back from doing whatever it was he was up to. The driver's side door was left ajar, and I pulled it open. I took a glance inside and spotted something on the seat that made my blood run cold. I picked it up and held the chess piece in the air.

"The Queen? And just what is that supposed to mean?"

I looked around me. The school parking lot was eerily quiet. A flock of pelicans floated above my head while my head spun with the many thoughts rushing through it. Where could he have gone? Why hadn't he taken his car?

Had something happened to William Covington? Had

something happened to him while I was supposed to have been protecting him?

## Chapter 40

*HELP!*

Jean had been in the trunk for what felt like an eternity. The car had stopped moving and had been parked somewhere for a long time while Jean was left in there for hours and hours. At first, she had tried to make noise and knock against the lid of the trunk, but the struggle had been so exhausting that she had fallen asleep at some point. As she woke up again, she was still in that small compartment, and fear spun through her body as she suddenly believed she had been left there so that no one would find her before she died from thirst or starvation.

*Please, someone, find me; Lord, please, help me!*

Jean kicked and moved around the little she could when she accidentally kicked the back of the compartment, and something came loose. A speck of light came in through the crack she had made in the old car, and she could peek into the cabin.

She heard noises from outside of the car, then lay completely still, barely breathing. She heard footsteps approaching, and someone was whistling. Then the door to the car opened and the radio was turned on again, music filling the car.

Jean squirmed up toward the crack she had made in the back seat and managed to peek into the cabin of the car. The person sitting behind the wheel was whistling along with the song on the radio, and the car took off down the road. The light blinded her slightly at first, but as soon as her eyes got used to it, she recognized the face of the doctor she had seen by Sophia's bedside.

Only this was no doctor.

The car took a turn, and Jean managed to squirm around even more, so she could get a better look. She then waited until the car came to another stop at a red light before she made her move. She kicked the seat hard, and it burst open. The driver still didn't hear anything over the loud music. It wasn't until Jean reached over the back of the seat and wrapped the rope used to tie her hands together around the driver's neck that she was finally seen.

A half-choked gurgling sound of surprise emerged from the driver's throat as Jean tightened the rope around the driver's neck. As the driver eased the foot on the brake, the car started to roll slowly forward into the intersection. The driver squirmed and fought for a few seconds before the body grew limp and lifeless. Jean managed to pull the body back into the back seat, then squirmed into the driver's seat, slid into position, and grabbed the wheel with her tied up hands, then placed both of her tied up feet on the brake just as the car was about to knock into a street sign.

Jean turned the car to the side, then managed to slide her tied up feet toward the accelerator and sped up. She maneuvered the car back onto the road and continued, then took a turn.

She drove the car through heavy Miami traffic while

people swerved around her, honking loudly, some giving her the finger, her mouth still gagged, her hands and feet still tied together. Then she found a parking lot in front of a school and drove into it and parked the car, breathing with relief.

She then turned her face to look at her attacker, lying lifeless in the backseat. She reached her hands up and tried to pull the gag out, but it still wouldn't move. Panting behind it, she squirmed across to the passenger seat and managed to open the glove compartment, then sighed with relief as she pulled out a fishing knife. Holding it between her two hands, she reached down and cut her feet loose. The rope used was thick, so she had to grind it for what seemed like forever.

Jean groaned behind the gag when finally, her feet came free, and she could move her legs properly again. She then had to turn the knife toward the rope holding her hands. It was a lot harder than she had expected, and the knife kept slipping out of her hands, but finally, she succeeded, and soon, she could move her hands again. She then lifted the knife to the rope strapped tight around her mouth and neck, holding the gag in place, then cut it, and finally could take out the nasty cloth. She spat and gagged as it was removed, suddenly feeling the pain in her jaw from being in the same position for hours and hours. She took a deep breath, then looked back at her attacker again. She turned around, reached into their pocket, and pulled out a cellphone.

She dialed a number, praying he'd pick up for once in his life.

## Chapter 41

I HAD BARELY GOTTEN BACK into the minivan when my phone rang. I pulled it out, then picked up.

"Hunter."

"I've seen the girl," a voice said on the other end. I recognized it immediately as T-Bone's.

"Lucy Lockwood?" I asked.

"Yes. She was just seen in Coconut Grove. I'll give you the address once we've negotiated a price."

"Coconut Grove? What's she doing there? That's where her parents live. Why would she go back there and risk being seen?"

"Listen, man; I don't know. But one of my buddies saw her drive into an address there and told me about it. If you want the address, then you have to pay up."

A million thoughts rushed through my mind in that instant. Lucy had been hiding out beach-side with the baby. If she had come back, it had to be important. It had to be worth the risk of being seen. But what could it be?

"William," I mumbled as my heart dropped. "Oh, my Lord."

"I want five big ones," T-Bone said. "For the information."

I grimaced. I didn't have five hundred dollars I could spare, especially not now that I was probably out of a job, and I wasn't sure Lucy's parents were going to pay up. I mean, the dad would probably do it, but I wasn't sure I wanted to tell him where his daughter and the grandchild he didn't know existed were—not after I saw the bruises on his wife.

"Listen, T-Bone, I am…"

"I get it. You don't have the money, do you?"

"Not really, but I do need to know where the girl is. It's very important. Can I owe you one?"

T-Bone laughed. "It's gotta be a big one then."

"It will be. I promise you."

"Okay. I'll hold you to that. You know, I will."

"I expect you to."

T-Bone sniffled. "All right. I'll text you the address."

We hung up, and I stared at the phone until the text arrived. I then glared at the address, startled, before I started the minivan back up and rushed down the street, cursing myself for not having seen this coming earlier.

I had made it to the neighborhood and approached the address when my phone rang again. I stared at the display. An unknown number, again.

I picked it up.

"Hello?"

"Hello…Harry?"

My heart dropped. "Jean? I…I haven't heard from you…where…I mean…what can I do for you?"

"Harry, I have something I need to tell you. It's urgent."

# Chapter 42

JEAN TOLD him everything she knew, everything Sophia had told her while mumbling in her sleep, a feeling of great relief rushing over her as she spoke.

"And you're sure about this?" Harry said, sounding somber. "Not that it surprises me. I had a hunch about this, but it's great to get it confirmed. It all makes a lot more sense now."

Jean sighed, exhausted. "That is good news. I hoped it would. I'm just glad I could be of help."

"So...where are you? I tried to call you?" Harry said. "You never picked up. I was...worried."

Jean felt her eyes fill as she thought about being kidnapped and held captive in the trunk. It was hard for her even to put it into words, as it still filled her with such profound fear.

"I...Sophia was attacked, and then...I tried to help her; I was..."

Jean stopped talking. Not because she didn't know what to say or how to say it or because it filled her with sadness and fear. No, it was because someone had taken the phone out of her hand. Now, Jean was staring at Sophia's attacker, holding the phone in their hand.

She could still hear Harry on the other end.

"Jean? Jean? Are you there? Jean?"

The attacker then reached over and slammed a fist into Jean's face so hard that she fell backward and hit her head into the door.

"JEAN?" Harry yelled somewhere in the distance, drifting slowly further and further away until she almost couldn't hear him anymore.

"What's going on, Jean?"

Jean wanted to answer, but she couldn't. She fought bravely to stay conscious as her attacker lifted the phone again and spoke into it.

"Jean can't talk now."

Her attacker then hung up and looked at Jean while she fought not to see double. The attacker then reached over, grabbed her by her collar, and pulled her closer, then lifted the fist again and slammed it into her face. Jean screamed as more punches fell. She pulled her arms up to cover her face, then lifted a leg and planted it in her attacker's stomach. The attacker flew backward with a shriek, and Jean reached for the handle of the door, then pulled it and opened the door. She crawled out, fighting to see straight, and was almost out when something grabbed her ankle and pulled her back. Jean screamed as she felt the hands on her leg, yanking her backward. When she was close enough, she turned around and placed a couple of fast punches on her attacker's jaw. The attacker screamed and let go of her leg, so Jean managed to slide out onto the asphalt, then kick the door of the car closed just before her attacker could follow her. She fought to get to her feet, then made a run for it. She could hear her pursuer opening the door with a loud grunt, then the footsteps behind her as the pursuit began. Jean screamed and sped up, running faster and faster, pushing herself. Luckily, Jean had always kept herself in good shape and was used to running on the beach. This was to her advantage now as she ran toward a strip mall. She turned a corner, thinking she had lost her pursuer, then spotted a family of four who had just parked their car and were walking up toward a Tropical Smoothie Café.

"Help," she hissed, but not loud enough for them to hear. She tried again, but it sounded mostly like wheezing. She turned her head to look behind her and could no longer see her pursuer. Happy about this, she sprinted to the end of the building where the parking lot started. Just as she came around the corner, someone stepped out in front of her. Startled, she let out a small scream to get the attention of the family across the parking lot, but her pursuer grabbed her, and with her mouth covered, she was dragged back toward the black Hyundai, crying and screaming, digging her nails into her attacker's skin.

## Chapter 43

"JEAN?"

I stared at the phone that had gone dead. I tried to call the number back, but it just kept ringing.

What had happened to her? Who was that person on the phone? Whose was that nasty voice?

Heart hammering in my chest, I kept staring at the phone, wondering what was happening. I had to help her somehow. What was it she said again? Before the phone was hung up?

*"Sophia was attacked and then...I tried to help her; I was..."*

She was what? Attacked? Kidnapped?

I leaned back in the seat of my car. "Oh, dear God, no. If anything happens to her, to Jean, I'll never forgive myself."

*Try and think clearly now. If Sophia was attacked, then Jean was most likely attacked by the same person, right? So, all this must have to do with what is happening to the girls at the school. It must be the same person who killed them who has taken Jean, right? And if that is so, then there is only one thing you can do, only one way to find Jean.*

I took a deep breath, then stared at the entrance to the mansion in front of me. I got out of the van, then walked up to the gate. Just as I did, a small Mercedes convertible came up to it. The window rolled down, and a hand pressed the buzzer and was let in. As the gate opened, I hid in the bushes, then as the car disappeared, I snuck in afterward just as it was about to close. I then walked up toward the house, stayed hidden by some palm trees and bushes until the young girl in the Mercedes stepped out and walked up to the main entrance, where she was let inside. I waited until the door was closed behind her and then a few seconds more before I snuck up to the house, ran around the back, and found a door that wasn't locked.

## Chapter 44

I FELT the gun in my holster and put my hand on the grip, then pulled it out as I walked down the marble-tiled hallway toward the voices coming from the dining room. The voices grew loud and angry the closer I got, and I recognized some of them.

"Okay, you've proven your point," one said. "You won."

Laughter followed. I knew that laugh a little too well.

*William.*

"No, no, my sweet girls. That's where you're wrong. It's not over yet."

"Please, William," another voice said.

*Lucy.*

"I thought you asked us to come here today to make a truce."

"You're the ones who wanted to meet," William said. "Not me. You texted me and picked me up at school, remember?"

"It has got to stop, William," Lucy continued. "You've taken it too far."

"I've taken it too far? Me?" William hissed. "Need I remind you what you did to me?"

They all went silent for a few seconds. I stayed hidden by the door, my gun ready.

"When is it ever going to end?" Lucy asked, her voice strained. "I'm sorry for what we did to you."

"I'm not," another voice said. I peeked inside and saw a girl I recognized from William's school. I had seen her in the mornings when we arrived. There were several of them present in William's living room. Some, I had seen before; others were new faces to me. But they all seemed to be about the same age.

The girl from earlier continued as she received looks from the others. "I'm not. He had it coming, and you all know it."

Another wave of silence brushed through the room, and I sensed the rest of the girls there agreed with her.

"It doesn't matter," Lucy said. "What matters is what happens next. William, you have got to stop this. Killing people won't solve this. Trying to make it look like I did it by placing stupid chess pieces on the bodies doesn't make anything better either. What will it take to make you stop?"

That made William stand to his feet. He walked toward Lucy and grabbed her around the shoulders, wearing that sly smile of his.

"You know what I want from you, dearest."

She shivered and pulled away from him. "I can't do that. You know I can't. Anything but that."

William grabbed her by the arm and pulled her back forcefully. He grabbed her around the neck and held her tight.

"That is my price. If you don't, the killings will continue."

William held Lucy tight around the neck, and I heard

her gasp for air. The other girls stood like they were frozen and stared at William as he tried to strangle Lucy. That was my cue. I had heard enough. I stepped forward, holding out the gun.

"No, they won't, William. It ends here. Let go of the girl. Let Lucy go. Now!"

## Chapter 45

"AH, DETECTIVE HUNTER," William said, grinning. "I was wondering when you'd join us. Did you like the little present I left for you in my car?"

I kept my gun pointed at him. He finally eased up on Lucy's neck.

"It's over, William," I said. "I heard everything. I know."

William scrutinized me. "Do you now?"

"Yes, I know what really happened at the beach last year. Sophia spilled the beans while she was in the hospital."

William's smile grew broader. "Did she really?"

Lucy's face grew pale. I looked at her.

"I realized it when I saw the baby. It was just a question of math, Lucy. If that child were a result of that rape, it wouldn't have been older than three months by now. But your baby sat up on her own when I arrived. She was teething. I have a child of my own and know that babies teethe at around six months old. It's also around the same age that they learn to sit by themselves. It was smart, though, to fake a rape to get back at him. And at the same time, you'd have an excuse to tell your parents how you got pregnant. So, you wouldn't have to tell them that you had slept with a teacher...with Mr. James."

"That's right, Detective," William said. "All these *good girls* were in on it. They all seem so innocent with their straight A's and volunteer work, but they did that to me. They planned this to get me sent to jail."

"And why did they do that, William? Because of what you did to them. You terrorized them. You forced Lucy to sleep with Mr. James, so you'd have something on him to be able to control him. You told her to do it, or you'd go to the immigration authorities and reveal that her mom was in the country illegally before she married Lucy's dad. Marriage is no longer a security from deportation in the times we live in. Not if you have been ordered deported before you were married. Lucy would do anything to protect her mother from being deported. And she did."

Lucy's eyes landed on the tiles beneath her, and she sat down in a recliner. Tears sprang to her eyes.

"It was the most humiliating I ever had to do. And now...now, I have a child."

"So, you decided to punish William for how he was treating everyone," I said. "All of the girls got together and agreed to stop him; am I right? Except you forgot a couple of things. First of all, when something like this happens in this day and age, there'll be video. From the beginning, it puzzled me that not one kid who had witnessed the rape had recorded it. It's nasty, but it would have happened. Second, when a young girl is raped, she's changed forever. When I met you at the apartment, you were strong and composed, not broken the way my sister was when it happened to her. That's when I began suspecting you had been lying."

"It's not like it was a total lie," another girl said. "He did rape someone. He raped a girl from school who didn't dare go to the police because her dad works for his dad, and she feared it might hurt her family. William knew this; that's why he picked her."

"So, you just faked one," I said. "On a girl who needed an excuse for her pregnancy. Bruised her up and left her in the sand to be found by her own father. Who made the call to Robert Lockwood, pretending to be William?"

"I did," a girl said. She had a deep voice, and it made sense that it could have been mistaken for a boy.

"But then when it came down to it, you didn't dare to testify, did you?" I asked. "You all backed out. You were supposed to tell what happened, to tell the police how you had seen William rape Lucy on the beach after the party. But you chickened out, didn't you, all of you?"

Eyes across the room avoided mine.

"I was scared," one of them said. "I'm sorry, Lucy, but I was terrified of what he might do to me. He came to me at school and threatened to kill me if I talked. Look what happened to Lisa, Georgiana, Sandra, Katelyn, and Martina. And what about Sophia?"

William laughed. "Look at you all. So pathetic."

I lifted the gun closer to his head. "That might be. But you're under arrest."

"For what?" he grinned.

"The murders of Lisa Turner, Sandra Barnes, Martina Hernandez, Katelyn Patterson, Georgiana Nelson, the attempted murder of Sophia Fischer, and the kidnapping of Jean Wilcox."

William stared at me, grinning even more.

"You think I did all that? I didn't kill anyone. No, you've got it all wrong, Detective. I didn't hurt any of them. I mean, I've wanted to, several times, but I didn't. Besides, murder isn't really my style. I prefer torturing people, seeing them suffer. That's my thing."

## Chapter 46

"WAIT. YOU DIDN'T KILL THEM?" Lucy said, standing to her feet again.

William shook his head. "You really need me to repeat it? No. I didn't. I didn't kill anyone. You just assumed that I did."

Lucy snorted. "Then why did you pretend like you were the killer just before when we asked you to stop?"

"Because it was fun," he said. "Thinking that I had killed your little friends gave me power over you. I enjoyed that, especially after what you did to me. I thought you deserved to fear me."

Lucy shook her head, narrowing her eyes. "You're a sick monster."

William laughed. "I'm not denying it. At least I know who I am, and I'm not afraid to show it."

I scrutinized him while trying to understand. Something was off here; something wasn't right. I lifted the gun again.

"Nope. I'm not buying it," I said. "You might not have

killed them, but you know who did. Why else would you put that chess piece in your car? You wanted me to think that it was Lucy. Just like the one who killed the other girls wanted me to think that too…to get back at her. She tried to frame you for rape and you—and whoever is killing for you—wanted her to go down for murder. And you know perfectly well who this person is, don't you, William?"

He shrugged. "Maybe I do; maybe I don't. What are you going to do about it, Detective? You're gonna arrest me and try to drag it out of me, huh? Is that what you're going to do? Take me down to the station and play tough guy?"

I walked closer, the gun pointed at him, then grabbed his arm and twisted it till he fell forward with his face against the dining table. I placed the gun to his head, then responded while smiling.

"Oh, I forgot to tell you. I was fired today. So, I guess I don't have anything to lose anymore, do I? I can act just as crazy as I want to."

That wiped the smirk off his face.

"Tell me who did the killings; tell me now," I said, pressing the gun into the back of his head.

William didn't answer. He whimpered slightly as I tightened my grip on his arm, pulling it up behind his back, hard.

"Tell me where Jean is."

Still, he said nothing. I pulled his arm again, and he screamed in pain. My hands were shaking in anger as I pressed the gun harder against his head, my finger uneasy on the trigger, ready to pull. I wanted to, boy; I wanted to finish him off right here and now. Two bullets. One for Reese, one for Jean. He could sense my eagerness to fire the gun. Still, the boy shut up like a clam, refusing to speak. But then he did something else that helped me. He glanced toward the kitchen for a brief second, and that was when it occurred to me.

*Of course.*

It all made sense now.

## Chapter 47

SHE WAS BEING PULLED by her hair. Jean screamed in pain as she was yanked forcefully across the floor.

"Stop, stop, please, just stop!"

As the pain finally eased up on her scalp, she felt her body plop down on the tiles and managed to look around. All she could make out was that she was in a kitchen some-where. Her attacker was doing something behind her back as Jean spotted a set of kitchen knives hanging on the wall and decided to make a run for them. Ignoring her aching body, she jumped to her feet and reached out her hand to grab one. But as she could feel it in her hand, her attacker grabbed her by the ponytail and pulled her back, hard.

Jean flew backward, screaming, and landed on the tiles. She slid across the floor until her back slammed against the wall. She looked down in her hand and realized she still had the knife. As her attacker stood above her, bending down, she lifted it. The knife slid through the skin on her attacker's cheek. Her attacker pulled backward with a shriek, then felt the cheek and the blood.

"What the…You…"

"Please, don't; please, don't hurt me anymore," Jean pleaded, trying to cover her face with her hands.

Her attacker tried to grab her, but she swung the knife again and cut her attacker on the upper arm. The sound of the knife going through the flesh made the hairs rise on her neck. Blood gushed out on the attacker's white shirt and dripped down on their white sneakers.

*I can't believe I just did that.*

Her attacker screamed in pain but didn't let go of Jean. A fist whistled through the air and landed on Jean's nose, then another on her cheek, while her attacker lifted her, then threw her across the room. As Jean landed, her attacker came down on her, ready to throw more punches. But somehow, Jean managed to swing the knife again and cut her attacker in the thigh. This one went deep, and she almost didn't get the knife back out. She had to pull really hard to keep the weapon in her hand.

Her attacker screamed, then felt the wound. Seconds later, more punches fell, and Jean kept cutting her attacker in the leg, then the arm, until her attacker finally managed to grab the arm that she was using for the knife, and bent it back so hard Jean dropped the knife. Her attacker then picked up the knife, turned it against her, and stabbed Jean. Jean screamed loudly. Her attacker grabbed the knife and pulled it out again, then raised it above Jean's chest. She swung it toward Jean when the door suddenly shattered to pieces, and someone stormed in. Next, a gun was placed to the attacker's head.

"Don't you even dare," sounded Harry's deep voice.

Jean felt a wave of great relief run through her as she saw his handsome face tower up behind her attacker. Harry stared at the woman holding Jean, his nostrils flaring, his eyes ablaze.

"You make one wrong move, and you're gone. Do you understand?"

## Chapter 48

DALISAY RAISED her hands in the air and let the knife fall to the tiles with a clang. She turned to look at me. Jean moaned and tried to move away from her attacker but was in too much pain. She had been stabbed in the leg and was losing blood, a lot of it.

Lucy came up behind me, then gasped as she saw Jean in a pool of blood.

"Call 911," I said. "Quick."

Lucy did. I heard her leave with the phone against her ear, talking to dispatch. I had Dalisay cuffed to a chair, then told one of the girls to keep an eye on her and let me know if she moved.

I took off my shirt and used it to try to stop the bleeding, but blood was gushing out, and Jean was turning pale. She didn't have long. It felt like the ambulance took forever to arrive.

"Harry...I...," she said, squirming in pain. Her eyes were matte and weak. My heart pounded in my chest. I wasn't losing her today.

"Shh," I said. "Don't say anything. We can talk later when you're better."

She grabbed my hand in hers. She squeezed it tight. I looked into her eyes and tried to calm her down, caressing her cheek gently. It was hard not to cry, seeing her like this and knowing it was all my fault.

"H-how?" she asked, looking into my eyes. "How did you know?"

I glanced at Dalisay, sitting on the chair. "Her tattoo. When she let me in the first time, I saw she had this tattoo on her arm by her wrist. I used to travel in the Philippines. I knew that tattoo was the mark of the Bahala Na Gang, a Philippine gang known for their brutality and terror regime in the country. When I found out it wasn't William who had killed them, I knew she was the only one here capable of murder. It suddenly all added up in a strange way. When I met her the first time, there was also something else that I noticed in her. She spoke to me in Filipino, but her dialect reminded me of how they spoke on an island I had visited when I traveled there. Jeju Island, where a community of women, some as old as eighty, goes diving ten meters under the sea to gather shellfish without the use of oxygen masks. Her dialect reminded me of them, and I guessed she grew up there. I knew the killer needed to have good diving skills and be more than an excellent swimmer. Finally, it was also something William's mother said when I first came here; she said that Dalisay took care of them all. That struck me as an odd choice of words, but I didn't make it out till just now. Dalisay would literally do anything for William, probably because he made her. She was the one who killed the girls, one after another. She also tried to run me off the road so William could use the fact that I wasn't on my post to get me off his back."

Jean tried to chuckle, but then something else

happened, something that terrified me to the core. Her eyes rolled back in her head, and her body went limp.

"No, Jean, no," I said, slapping her cheeks to try and wake her. "Don't you dare leave me now, Jean! JEAN!"

I shook her, trying to wake her, but she was gone. Panic erupted inside me. Suddenly, I was taken back to that day, years ago, when I held Camille in my arms the very same way, shaking her, screaming her name as she hung lifeless in my arms. My heart felt like it was going to explode as I relived everything from that terrifying day. I screamed her name, while I frantically shook her, tears spilling from my eyes.

"Don't do this to me, Jean. Don't you dare leave me too."

## Chapter 49

I WAS STILL in the waiting room at the hospital when Fowler came to see me. He wasn't exactly who I wanted to see at this point, but he didn't seem to come here to fight. He didn't have that look in his eyes as he walked closer. He sat down in a chair next to me, then gave me half a smile before asking:

"How's she doing? Any news?"

I shook my head. My nails were almost gone. I could still barely breathe. So much of this reminded me of when I brought in Camille. I never thought I'd find myself in this position again. It scared me like nothing else. Would I ever get to see Jean again? The thought of losing another woman I loved was unbearable.

"Nothing," I said, my voice shivering. "It's been hours."

Fowler nodded and gave me a sympathetic look. "We took the maid in and are in the process of interrogating all the girls. What a story this is turning out to be. It's a terrible mess."

"And William Covington?" I asked.

"That's why I came," Fowler said. "He wasn't there when we arrived. He must have escaped at some point in all the chaos."

I stomped my feet in agitation. "No! Argh, it's all my fault. I was so focused on Jean that I didn't keep an eye on him. How could I have been so stupid!"

Fowler placed a hand on my shoulder. "It's okay. We'll get him. The girls are finally talking, telling us everything he's been up to. We're getting a lot of stuff on him. He's still just a young kid; he can't have gone far."

I exhaled tiredly and rubbed my face. "You don't know William very well, then. He's capable of a lot of things."

"We'll get him. I've put up roadblocks all over town, and we have searches out everywhere. He can't leave town without me knowing; be certain of that. If he as much as farts, I'll know about it."

I nodded with a deep exhale. "I sure hope you're right. I wouldn't be able to stand it if he got away with what he has done. He's slippery like a snake, never getting his own hands dirty. Is the maid talking?"

"Not a word," Fowler said. "But we'll get her to."

"I sure hope so. Get her to tell everything, especially how William got her to kill for him."

Fowler smiled and blinked. "There's the detective I know so well. Determined and relentless. Welcome back."

He patted me on the back with a laugh.

"I missed you, bro. I knew you could solve this case."

I lifted both eyebrows. "Did you now?"

"Never doubted it for a second. Morales and his team are good, but who am I kidding? They couldn't catch a killer like that. Once Jean is better, and you've rested for a bit, then come to see me. I'm putting you back in homicide."

I nodded and gave him half a smile. "Thanks. I appreciate it."

Fowler rose to his feet with a sigh. "Now, I have to get back. Lots of work to be done in the coming days. Let me know when you hear news, okay? We're all rooting for her."

"Thanks, Fowler. That means a lot to me."

He left, and I was once again all alone in the waiting room, sitting in the uncomfortable chairs, waiting. I closed my eyes, then slid off the chair and onto my knees, folding my hands. I remembered sitting in that very same position when Camille was fighting for her life and then realizing that she had survived yet suffered brain damage. I remembered how angry I got at God after that. I hadn't prayed like this since.

"Please, dear God, let Jean live," I said. "I know it's selfish, but I need her. I know I've been angry with you. I was so mad at you when you took Camille away. I felt like it was a cruel joke. You let her live like I prayed about, yet she never really came back to me. This time, I pray that Jean will survive and that she'll recover and be herself fully. Please, dear God, don't take her away from me too...I beg..."

I was still on my knees, literally, when the doors opened, and the doctor came into the room. I rose to my feet, heart hammering against my rib cage as I walked to him, just as I had done three years ago when I received the news about Camille.

"Doctor?"

I swallowed, pressing back my tears. So many bad memories, so much fear and anxiety I had to face at this moment; it was overwhelming.

*If she doesn't make it, I don't know what I'm going to do.*

"She's going to be fine, Detective," he said with a soft

smile. "She lost a lot of blood, but she's no longer in critical condition. She's gonna be okay. You can breathe again."

## Chapter 50

IT WAS late before I got home. I walked inside and found my dad sleeping in the recliner, the TV running loudly. He woke up as I slammed the door shut.

"Harry?"

He sat up straight and turned off the TV.

"She'll be fine," I said. "I even got to talk to her briefly before she had to go to sleep. I stayed for a little while to make sure she was good."

My dad pulled me into a deep hug, then patted me on the shoulder. His worried eyes lingered on me, and he tried to hide it behind a smile. He, too, had been concerned about Jean, no doubt about it. He was very fond of her.

"Da-a-ad!"

Josie came tumbling down the stairs and threw herself into my arms. "How is she?"

"Like I texted you earlier, she'll be fine. But she's tired. She's lost a lot of blood. She told me to tell you that she misses you, though, and she'll be back as soon as possible."

"Were you scared, Daddy?"

"I was, sweetie. I really was."

"I was praying for her, Daddy," she said.

"That's why she's fine," I said. "God listens to you. Now, go and get ready for bed."

Josie's smile vanished. "Could you tuck me in tonight? I got really scared when I heard about Jean."

That made me smile. Josie hadn't wanted me to tuck her in for a long time since she felt she was too old for that now. I poked her nose.

"You betcha. Now, go, get ready."

She kissed my cheek, then ran up the stairs, and I turned to face my dad, suddenly feeling the exhaustion and hunger from a very long and intense day.

"There's pizza on the counter," my dad said like he read my mind.

I grabbed a piece and bit into it, then went for a beer in the fridge and opened it. I sank into the couch next to my dad with a deep sigh, eating my pizza, and drinking my beer. Later, I tucked my daughter in, and, as my dad left, I went to our bedroom and sat by Camille, then told her everything that had happened that day.

I must have dozed off in the chair because, when I woke up, the clock by the window said three a.m. I felt sore from sleeping in a chair and moved my upper body when I heard a noise. It sounded like someone struggling. It came from across the hallway.

*Josie!*

I sprang to my feet and stormed toward her room. The door was ajar, and inside, I saw a shadow move. I opened the door completely.

"Josie? Are you all right?"

Inside, I saw something that made my heart stop.

"William?"

He had pulled Josie out of bed and was holding his

arm around her neck in a tight grip. He held a gun to her head.

"Dad?" she whimpered.

I reached out my hand toward them. "William, don't do anything stupid. We can talk about this."

"One step closer, and she dies," William said, speaking through gritted teeth. He had a look in his eyes that told me he was desperate enough to kill her if he had to.

"What do you want?" I asked. "I assume you didn't come here to kill my daughter. You want something from me, am I right? Put the gun down, and we'll talk."

William grinned, but he didn't put down the gun. "I do need something from you. You're right about that," he said. "But, I'm going to do the talking, and you'll listen."

"I am listening," I said. "Just, please, don't hurt her. What do you need?"

"I can't get out of this town since they have these darn roadblocks everywhere. I need you to help me get out of here. You help me, and I might let her live."

## Chapter 51

"I CAME HERE ON FOOT," William said. "I don't have any means of transportation."

We had walked outside my townhouse. He was still holding Josie tightly, the gun to her head.

"All I have is a motorcycle," I said. "The minivan I drove while protecting you belonged to the police department, and they took it back while I was at the hospital. I took a taxi home."

"Don't detectives have unmarked cars?" William asked.

"Yes, but mine broke down two weeks ago."

"I guess we're going on a bike ride, then," he said. "Let's go."

I took the bike out and got on it. William approached, still holding Josie. I shook my head when realizing what his plan was. My daughter realized it too.

"Da-ad?"

"No, no, we can't ride this with more than two people," I said.

He gave me a suspicious look. "Of course, we can. The girl takes up no space."

"It's too dangerous," I said. "Not to mention illegal. The police will stop us if they see us."

"So, you'll outrun them. You're faster than they are. I'm not letting go of her. She's my security that you'll do as I tell you. I'm not letting her go."

"Dad?" Josie said, whimpering.

I shook my head. There was no way I could allow this. I usually never allowed Josie on the bike. It was too dangerous, especially with three people on it. If we crashed, Josie would most surely die. I didn't even have enough helmets for three people.

But William wasn't going to budge.

He stared at me, pressing the gun against Josie's head. "Either we all get on that bike, or she dies. It's your choice."

I exhaled, terrified. "All right. All right. But at least give her your helmet."

"No way," he said and urged Josie to get on the bike behind me. She reached her arms around my waist and hugged me, then leaned her head against my back. I could feel how her body was shaking with fear.

I took off my helmet and handed it to Josie. "Here, put that on, and hold on tight. It might get bumpy."

## Chapter 52

MY BIKE ROARED to life underneath me, and we soared into the dark night, my worried heart pounding in my chest as I swung the bike out onto the road. Josie held onto me tightly and hid her face behind my back. I wanted to comfort her so badly, to take her in my arms and tell her it would all be fine, that soon everything would be okay again. But I couldn't. I knew William probably had the gun pressed against her back, and she had to be beyond terrified.

"There's a roadblock coming up at the end of this road," I said as we had reached the end of 19$^{th}$ Avenue and turned down Flagler Street, driving past the seafood market where I used to take Camille when we were younger.

"What do you want to do?"

"Show them your badge. Don't they know you?" he asked.

"Doesn't matter," I said. "They'll never let us through with three people on a bike."

"Take another road," he said. "One that doesn't have a roadblock."

"I don't know all the roadblocks, if that's what you think," I yelled through the noise from my bike.

"Do it anyway."

I did as he told me to and swung down 22$^{nd}$ Avenue. There was no roadblock, so we continued further down 22nd until we reached Dixie. William told me to speed up, so I did, hoping that a patrol car would see us and stop us. I rode past a place where I knew a patrol usually kept an eye out, and I was right. It was there, as usual. I roared past the car, speeding excessively past it, making as much noise as I possibly could.

It worked. Seconds later, the cruiser followed.

"Shoot," William said. "They're following us. Lose them!"

"I'm going as fast as I can," I yelled back.

I felt the gun pressed against my neck. "I don't think you are."

"It's dangerous to go faster," I said. "I risk killing us all if we crash."

"I'm willing to take that risk," William said. "Are you willing to risk your daughter's life?"

I exhaled and took another glance at the police cruiser behind me, almost catching up to us.

"I am sorry," I said, then sped up, and seconds later, I saw the cruiser become smaller and smaller in the mirror. I bit down on my lip, trying to press my fears away, then roared forward, taking a turn a little too sharply, not taking into account the extra weight I was carrying, making it harder to turn. The bike skidded sideways, and Josie screamed, but I accelerated just in time to get it around the corner without losing our balance or control. I got it back and running, then ran it down another street when we saw blinking lights in the distance.

"Another roadblock," I said, going fast toward it. "What do you want to do?"

William looked behind us, where the cruiser was still trying to catch us. It was now joined by two other patrol cars that came from side streets.

"What do you want to do, William?" I yelled.

"I'm thinking!" he yelled back.

"Gotta think fast! It's coming up!"

"Go through," he then said. "Drive right through the roadblock!"

I swallowed hard. I was afraid he was going to say that.

"All right," I said and accelerated as we came closer and closer to the block. "Hold on, Josie!"

The officers behind the block were yelling at us, but I couldn't hear anything. Then I saw them jump for their lives as they realized I wasn't going to stop. I slammed the motorcycle right into the barricade. When we hit the barricade, William was slung into the air. He flew into one of the parked cars and crashed into it.

I lost control of the bike, and it tilted to the side, then skidded across the asphalt, Josie screaming behind me until we finally came to a stop. Completely out of it, I tried to figure out what was up and what was down, then spotted Josie lying on the asphalt behind me. Blood was running from my legs, and I was in pain, but it didn't matter. All that mattered was her. While police surrounded William with guns, I crawled to my daughter and reached out my hand to touch her shoulder and turned her around.

"Josie," I whispered, then yelled: "Josie!"

# ONE WEEK LATER

## Chapter 53

"I'VE GOT another one ready. Who's the taker?"

Josie raised her hand in the air, the one that wasn't bandaged. My dad placed the patty on her plate. We were in the backyard of my townhouse. It was a nice seventy-three degrees out, and, as true Floridians, we believed that was perfect for barbecuing, even if we were at the beginning of February.

Josie grabbed a bun, then made her burger and ate it with one hand. She had been lucky and had just broken her arm, along with receiving a lot of scrapes and bruises. Nothing that wouldn't heal eventually, as the doctor had put it.

I had been lucky myself. Nothing was broken, but lots of road rash and a burn on my arm. My dad said we had guardian angels to protect us.

William had survived, too, but was in critical condition. They were doing all they could to keep him alive, so he could stand trial. Fowler and his crew were building a case against him, and it was beginning to look promising. More than twenty people had come forward so far to tell

ALL THE GOOD GIRLS

what he had done, and they were all prepared to testify in court against him. Sophia was one of them. She had woken up and was ready to talk, even though she knew it meant getting in trouble for what they had tried to do to him. She and Lucy had both agreed to tell the entire truth. My colleagues had even gotten Dalisay to admit that William had pressured her to make those kills. Dalisay had a sick mother who was dependent on the money she sent back to the Philippines. Dalisay had earlier stolen a pile of cash from William's mother's drawer, and William recorded her doing it with his phone. He promised to keep quiet only if she promised to do everything he said. If she went to jail, her mother wouldn't survive without the money that she sent home. Now, she was going to jail for what she had done for a lot longer than if she had just been punished for taking the money. Hopefully, she was taking William down with her. I had great faith that he would be going down for a very long time. His parents had cut him off, so there were no more expensive lawyers to fight for him. It was time he paid his dues.

"I'll have a hot dog if you have one," Jean said. She was sitting in a lawn chair, a set of crutches leaning against her chair. She had been home for a couple of days, and we were finally beginning to feel like ourselves again.

"This is so much better than hospital food," she said, her mouth full of the last hot dog that she had barely started to swallow before she asked for another one.

My dad handed her one, and she smiled, then put it in a bun and bit into it. I had a burger like my daughter and plastered it with ketchup. It was my second burger, so I was getting there, but still felt like there might be room for a hot dog as well.

After we were done eating, Josie ran back inside to play

173

on her computer, while my dad said he'd go watch some TV.

Jean and I were finally alone. We hadn't been since the day of the kiss. And we hadn't talked about it. It was about time.

"Listen…Harry…" she started. "About that kiss, I don't know why I…I mean, I know you can't, of course, you…"

I stopped her. She looked up, and our eyes locked.

"I think it's time I move on," I said.

"What?"

I exhaled and took her hands in mine. "I have given this a lot of thought, and my dad is right; I need to enjoy my life. Camille would want me to. She wouldn't want me to sit here and whither."

"What are you saying, Harry?"

"I'm going to put Camille in a nursing home. I've already taken a look at some here in the area. I can visit as much as I want. She'll have care twenty-four-seven, and I won't have to always depend on you and my dad. I'm back in homicide, and they actually expect me to show up to the briefings and such. I think it's time for me to focus on my job if I want to keep it."

"Sounds smart," Jean said. "But a tough decision."

"The hardest I've ever had to make. But I think she'll be happy there, as happy as she can be. They can give her what she needs. But this also means that…"

I paused because it was hard to say.

"Yes?"

"That we could…maybe try to…I mean…how about we start by dating? How do you feel about that?"

Jean looked at me, then smiled. "I would like that very much, Harry."

"I realized this when I almost lost you, Jean. But I think I could possibly love you; maybe I already do."

Jean smiled again, then leaned over and placed her lips against mine. She caressed my cheek gently and looked into my eyes. A tear escaped her eye and rolled down her cheek. She parted her lips as if to speak, but I placed a finger on them, then kissed her instead. As our lips parted again, we heard a scream coming from inside the house.

"Josie!"

I stood to my feet and rushed to the back porch, then ran inside. Jean came up behind me, humping along on her crutches.

"Josie?" I called once inside. "What's going on? Why are you screaming?"

Josie came down the stairs. She looked like she had seen a ghost.

"What's wrong, Josie?" Jean asked as she came in behind me, panting.

Josie stood like she was frozen at the top of the stairs. "I...I...I wanted to check on Mom and then..."

"Is something wrong with Mom?" I asked, my heart hammering in my chest. My dad came in from the living room and stood in the doorway.

"No...I mean...yes, I think so."

I ran up the stairs while Jean humped up after me, taking a little longer on her crutches. "What's wrong with Mom, Josie?" I asked, holding her shoulders between my hands.

"I was sitting with her, holding her hand in mine, singing that old song, you know the one we used to sing before bedtime when suddenly...she...she looked at me, Dad. She lifted her head and looked directly at me!"

"She did what?"

"I think you should look for yourself," she said and pointed at the door.

I didn't think about it twice. I grabbed the door and opened it. Behind it, I was met by the sweetest sight I had ever seen in my life. Camille's beautiful brown eyes were looking directly at me. I gasped, startled, then stood and stared at her for a long time, trying to figure out whether I was dreaming or not. So many nights and days, I had sat by her bedside and dreamt that she'd suddenly look at me, suddenly wake up.

"She also spoke, Dad. She said my name. At least, it sounded like she said it," Josie squealed excitedly.

Camille stared at me, blinking. Then her lips parted, and a whistling noise emerged from between them, shaping a word:

"Josie."

I just about lost it. I gasped for air, my heart hammering in my chest. "Oh, my God, Camille, you're awake. I have never...I never..."

"It's...a miracle," my dad said, coming inside. "Just like you said, remember? You told me you still believed it would happen, even though the doctors said it wouldn't, and now...look at this?"

"She's awake, Dad; look, she's looking at you, see it, Daddy?" Josie said, almost screaming.

"I can't...I can't believe it," I said and took her hand in mine, tears spilling from my eyes. As I looked across the room, my eyes fell on Jean, who was still standing in the hallway, and my heart dropped instantly. Seeing this, Jean turned around and walked away. Startled, I stood for a few seconds, not knowing what to do, then let go of Camille's hand, and ran out after her.

"Jean."

She stopped at the top of the stairs. She didn't turn to look at me.

"I'm...I'm..."

She turned to face me, tears in her eyes. "You're what? Sorry? How can you be? This is what we prayed for over three long years. This is what we wanted, Harry. Josie has her mother back; you have your...wife. You can be a family again. This is a good thing, Harry. Go. Be with your family. I'll catch you all later."

"But..."

"Harry, go."

I felt awful, yet so confused. I turned around and ran back into our bedroom, where my daughter was sitting on the bedside, crying her little heart out. Camille was just staring at her, whispering her name. I grabbed both of them in my arms and pulled them into a deep hug, hoping I would never have to let go again. As we hugged, I heard the front door slam shut. My heart ached for Jean, but I tried so hard not to think about it. I closed my eyes and decided to enjoy the moment. Jean was right. This was what I wanted. This was what I had dreamt of happening for three years. It was the best ending to a terrible journey for all of us. Now, we could finally begin the healing process. We could finally become a family again.

My prayers had finally been answered.

THE END

Want do know what happens next?
Get Book 2 in the **Harry Hunter** Mystery Series,
***RUN GIRL RUN*** here:
mybook.to/run-girl

# Afterword

Dear Reader,

Thank you for purchasing *All the Good Girls* (Harry Hunter #1). This is the first book in a planned series of shorter, more fast-paced mysteries. I loved writing this story, and I hope you enjoyed reading it as well. I hope to write many more books about Harry Hunter.

As usual, some of the things in this story are taken from the real world. The rape in the beginning was inspired by a real rape that happened at a high school dance, where tons of kids saw it happen, and the guy even called the dad afterward.

You can read more here if you want to.

https://www.huffpost.com/entry/richmond-high-gang-rape-victim_n_3389573

The story of the Philippine gang and the divers on Jeju Island is real too. You can read about these amazing women here:

https://ich.unesco.org/en/RL/culture-of-jeju-haenyeo-women-divers-01068

Thank you for all your support. Don't forget to leave a review if you can.

Take care,
Willow Rose

## About the Author

Willow Rose is a multi-million-copy best-selling Author and an Amazon ALL-star Author of more than 70 novels.

Several of her books have reached the top 10 of ALL books on Amazon in the US, UK, and Canada. She has sold more than three million books all over the world.

She writes Mystery, Thriller, Paranormal, Romance, Suspense, Horror, Supernatural thrillers, and Fantasy.

Willow's books are fast-paced, nail-biting page turners with twists you won't see coming. That's why her fans call her The Queen of Scream.

Willow lives on Florida's Space Coast with her husband and two daughters. When she is not writing or reading, you will find her surfing and watch the dolphins play in the waves of the Atlantic Ocean.

To be the first to hear about **exclusive new releases and FREE ebooks from Willow Rose**, sign up below to be on the VIP List. (I promise not to share your email with anyone else, and I won't clutter your inbox.)